WASHAKA
The Bear Dreamer
by Jamie Lee

A Lakota story
based on Leon Hale's dream

Many Kites Press

Rapid City, South Dakota

A Many Kites Press Book
Copyright © 2006 Jamie Lee

Many Kites Press
3907 Minnekahta Dr.
Rapid City, SD 57702
www.manykites.com

Original story told by Leon Hale

Cover Illustration by Rusty Speidel

Library of Congress Control Number
2005936108

ISBN-13   978-0-97290-024-9
ISBN-10   0-9729002-4-1

High schools, colleges, universities and reading groups may wish to purchase this book wholesale to generate discussions on race and place in the United States. For wholesale or discount information call 1-800-486-8940.

Printed in the United States by Morris Publishing
3212 East Highway 30
Kearney, NE 68847
1-800-650-7888

Dedicated to:

Leon and Priscilla Hale
for allowing me to write this story,

And to Little Leon,

And to Milt,
for not letting me toss one more
manuscript into the abyss

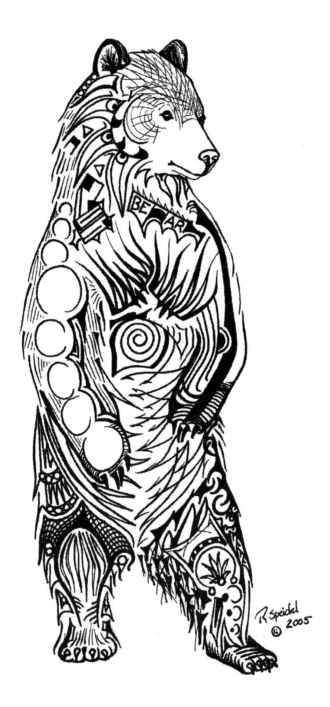

Author's Introduction

It was the edge of winter 2005 and I was casting about looking for a new story idea. I like to write in coffee shops and was sitting near a window scribbling in a notebook when an Indian man about my age came to my table and asked if I was a writer. I nodded to him and said, yes. He introduced himself as Leon Hale and asked if he could sit and tell me a story. We shook hands, and he began.

Leon told me about a dream he has had for many years. It is always the same dream; full of rich detail, sounds, smells, and sights. In the dream, he is a young Lakota boy living in a tipi village in the early 1800s just as the huge westward migration of Europeans into Indian country was beginning. Leon said that sometimes when he wakes up and finds himself a grown man living in a trailer house, he is disoriented and confused.

Within minutes, I knew I would write his story.

Over the next few months, Leon came to my house and we recorded his dream. He'd sit in my green leather chair, go into what appeared to be a deep trance, and speak in first person about his life as a young Lakota living on the plains. I usually stretched out on my couch and went into a trance-like state myself. It took eleven sessions to record his story. He feels his dream comes from that time and is *Wakan*—sacred—and needs to be in the world.

Later, he told me that during a serious illness, his grandson, Little Leon, used to come over and urge him to get up and walk, to be *washaka*, to be strong. They would walk and Leon would tell him the stories of Little Chief. Little Leon told his grandfather that one day he would write these stories—or pray to *Wakan Tanka* that they would find a writer who could write the stories.

Writing *Washaka—The Bear Dreamer* was a great pleasure for me. I took the bare bones of Leon's dream and added flesh, characters, story and, I hope, heart.

While writing this story, I struggled with how to place it within known events in Lakota country and finally realized it must simply be told in the way that Leon "captured" it. As a reader, please take Leon's story as it comes; in the form of a dream, in its spirit. The Crazy Horse and Sitting Bull of this story precede the historic figures by a generation. And that is how we offer *Washaka—The Bear Dreamer* to you.

Note: The Lakota language is a beautiful and ancient language and today many people work hard to keep it a viable language. We have used a few Lakota words when appropriate. Most are clearly read. The name *Mato Ska* is pronounced *Matoshka*. *Mato* means bear and *Ska* means white. *Wasaka* is pronounced similarly as *Washaka* and means the strong one. We have used the phonetic spelling of the word within the title to assist people in pronouncing it. One day we hope to have the entire story translated into Lakota to support the preservation of this beautiful language.

Acknowledgments
I would like to acknowledge my husband, Milt Lee, for his continual support of my writing life. Thanks to my three favorite editors, Andi Hummel, Gaydell Collier and Chris Christopherson for helping to shape and polish this story, and to The Spearfish Writers and The Bearlodge Writers for taking me in. Additional thanks go to my students at Oglala Lakota College for acting as first readers; their warm response inspired me to move ahead.

And finally, love to my grandchildren, Gavin, Jaaron, Korah, and Kelsey, and to the granddaughter of my heart, Kayna. Without the children, there is no future.

Table of Contents

Ash

When a man's body is raised high on a scaffold and burned, skin and hair and bone blacken, crumble, and become ash. The ash is lifted, carried by wind high above the earth and scattered.

I am ash now.

The day my body burned, the wind was blowing east and it carried me aloft, lifting and lifting until the sun warmed the ash, and the rain washed me back to earth

Ash has eyes and memory; spirit lingers in ash. When my body burned, I was freed from all physical restraint, free to fly like eagles and birds, free to mingle with earth and water, to nourish the grasses and plants, to be eaten by deer and bear and wolf.

When my body burned and became ash, I was no longer tethered by human limitation but liberated, turned loose amidst the world, free to roam, to watch, to cross previously unseen boundaries between life and death, to be breathed in by *Wakan Tanka,* the Great Spirit. I am still here.

I was even free to be reborn a hundred years later into the body of a boy in Thunder Butte, to ease myself into his dreams, to have him remember my story and tell it to others.

1 The *Lakota Oyate*—The People

The first time I heard about the Others, the different kind of people, I was in my seventh year. It was the edge of summer. The days had been blistering hot and dry for weeks, but suddenly the season shifted toward fall and the nights grew cool, the air scented with the smell of the coming winter. Our village was camped beside a thin, clear stream on the eastern edge of *He Sapa*, the hills of black. We'd been here since late spring and the men were preparing to hunt the buffalo.

My name then was Little Chief, *Itancan Cikala*. My mother called me "Little Mischief." It was my nature to be busy from the time the sun rose in the morning until it dropped out of the sky again. Grandfather Whirling Hand called me "curious."

The best part of every day was when the other boys and I gathered in Grandfather's tipi to hear his stories. I never thought about where the girls were—I guess they were in Grandmother's tipi. I loved Grandfather's stories, even the ones I'd heard a hundred times before. I'd race through my evening chores and bolt to his tipi to help with his chores so we could get to the stories sooner.

Sometimes he'd refuse to let me in until I went to wash in the stream—said I smelled like a sweaty dog and he couldn't bear the scent of me. Grandfather was like that.

He never held back words, but he could say I stunk and it hit me gentle-like, not harsh or cruel.

So that is how it was, the edge of summer—hot, flies buzzing, sun beating down during the day and the earth cooling and growing damp during the night. When Grandfather told the story about the Others, it was a night like this.

I was already in the tipi, my body clean as a river rock, when my little cousins came in carrying small stones and other things they'd found that day. They liked bringing their finds to Grandfather—he always made up a story about each object and what it meant. He said rocks and trees and bones all had spirit, and that these spirits spoke to him. Usually the stones and sticks had something to tell us about growing stronger, not whining, helping the women more. I knew he made up the stories to teach us. Grandfather was the oldest man in our village. Nobody knew how old—not even Grandfather. He was my father's father's father, which actually made him my great-grandfather.

During these times, all the children—including me—listened to every word. Grandfather told of how the world was formed from *Inyan*, his blood flowing in blue rivers to form sky and water until he himself turned to stone. He also told stories about coyote and bear and stars, and the early travels of our people. My favorite story told of our emergence from the body of *Unci Maka*, Grandmother Earth, after the second cleansing.

The night I heard the story of the Others, there were nine of us in a circle in Grandfather's tipi. I always sat opposite him because I liked watching his face across the small fire. The curls of smoke looked like spirit fingers touching his nose and brow, and then rising up and out of the tipi hole. Grandfather's face was smooth and brown, as soft as finely-tanned leather. He hardly ever smiled but, when he did, his eyes crackled like lightning in a stormy sky.

I was the oldest of the children in our camp and *tanhansi* Rabbit, my cousin, sat next to me. He and I were the same age and always together. Our fathers were brothers and we treated each other as brothers, too. That night we'd built a fire because Grandfather said his bones were stiff. The children laughed at him, saying bones are always stiff. There was a lot of laughter and joking around, but I just sat and poked at the logs with a thin, burning stick. Outside it was cold, but inside it was warm and dim as a cave.

I watched the flames, watched the smoke curl up like ghostly fingers, watched Grandfather's face. A log snapped in the crackling fire as if signaling silence and we all went quiet. He began with a prayer to *Wakan Tanka* to guide his words and his stories, and to make our ears work. We waited for Grandfather to finish his *wacekiya*, his praying, and begin the storytelling.

When he finished, he looked straight across the fire at me and said, "Tonight, a story for you, Little Chief."

That was the first time the shiver passed through my body. At the time I thought it was the cold night air, but it was more than that. I sat up straight, excited about having a story directed at me. I had no idea his words that night would change my life.

Grandfather began, "It was the summer you were born. Your mother was large with you, and we had made camp to the south of here. It was a difficult summer; the game had been hiding, and the hunters were often gone for days at a time in search of elk and deer. The buffalo hunt had not yet begun."

A birthing story, I thought. We all loved hearing stories about how each of us had come into the world. I figured Grandfather was going to tell the story of my birthing day once again; how I'd had slipped into the world like a wet seed just as the sun topped the horizon, how my father had awakened the entire camp with his jubilant calls and cries, how Father carried me to Grandfather as if I were a small, slick buffalo calf.

On this night however, instead of birthing stories, he had a different story to tell. "A few days before you were born, Little Chief, your father and uncle went south to hunt. They came upon a small river. There was steam rising from the surface of that river. They got off their horses and put their hands in to feel the hot water, having heard of these hot streams but never finding one before. They decided to swim."

I listened. His voice was like a river song, words tumbling like water over stones.

Grandfather went on. "There was a place where the water fell over an edge of rock and formed a small pool. Your father and uncle tied their horses to a nearby tree and were about to jump in when they saw a small mule deer standing in the woods. It was alert, rigid, its eyes fixed and staring in the opposite direction. The deer didn't see them. They wondered what had caused the deer to freeze, as if afraid. They grabbed their bows and arrows, preparing for unseen danger and hoping to take down the deer—their bellies were rumbling." Grandfather grinned. "A hungry man is always a good hunter."

The children laughed, but I shivered again, waiting to hear more. "Go on, Grandfather," I urged him.

"*Takoja*, Grandson, I think you are in a hurry for this story." He smiled and went on. "The deer skipped off before they could notch an arrow. Then they heard clanging and banging in the distance, a sound unfamiliar and out of place on the quiet land. They took their bows and arrows and followed the hot stream toward the sound. When they got close, your uncle climbed a tree to search for where such a noise was coming from. And that is when your uncle saw the Others."

Grandfather paused, his eyes rose and looked out the tipi hole as if sending a prayer to the heavens, and then he went on. "Your uncle saw something built from wood plank sitting in a meadow with large wheels lifting it off the ground. It was covered with cloth, like a rounded tipi, or a sweat lodge. A team of horses was hitched to this wagon and a man was leading the team. The man was different from us; pale, his face covered with hair, his eyes shaded by a hat on his head, his body covered in cloth with chunky moccasins on his feet.

All of this your uncle whispered down from the tree from where he watched. Your father climbed up to see for himself what was being described. Atop the cart was a woman who, like your mother, was large with child. She was also pale—her hair yellow as the prairie grass in the last days of summer. Never had your father and uncle seen such a sight."

I still held the burning stick in my hand. Something about Grandfather's story was like that burning stick; it touched my mind the way a spark touches dry grass. I felt suddenly hot and cold at the same time. I tried to form a picture of what he described, but couldn't. Curiosity shot through me. I wanted to see these Others. I wanted to see what my father and uncle had seen. The world seemed to tilt off its center. Other people? Different people? Hairy faces, and chunky moccasins, and rolling wagons, and—

"What was the sound they heard, Grandfather?"

"The man was building something. Your father and uncle did not wait to see what it was he was building. They scooted down from the tree and returned to the village to tell us what they had seen."

The younger children in the tipi were getting restless, waiting for a new story, but Grandfather was not done yet.

"I have heard of these Others," he said. "My grandfather had a vision. So have other Elders. They said that one day Others would come, many Others, and that life would change for us."

He looked at me, his face serious. "When your father and uncle returned, we moved camp further north, to stay away from the Others. But before we broke camp, they returned once more to the steaming river. The man and his wife were still there. They were cutting trees, pulling the bark from the logs, stacking the logs; they were building a home."

"Where were their people?" I asked. "Did the woman have her baby? How could these people get enough food without their band? How could they live? Where did they come from?"

In the dim firelight, Grandfather's smile looked sad to me. He shook his head and said, "I cannot answer all your questions, Little Chief, except to say that our Elders from long ago saw this, that these wagons would bring a different kind of people to our lands, and that there would be many challenges, many changes for the *Lakota Oyate*. That is all we know. You, Little Chief, were born the day after your father returned."

That night I had a fever. It was as if I'd carried the fire of the story with me. The buffalo robe beneath me felt scratchy and rough. I rolled and rolled and couldn't sleep. Mother crossed the tipi and put her cool hand on my forehead. "Shh, *cinksi*, my son. You will awaken your father." She lay down beside me and her body stilled the shivering in my limbs.

"Mother, did Father tell you about seeing the Others?"

"Yes, son. He talked of nothing else for weeks after your birth."

"Why has he never told me about them?"

"Little Chief, you are still a child. These are matters better left to the men. It was not your business. Go to sleep now, *cinksi*."

I soon heard the soft sound of her breathing, but still my body did not rest. It hurt to be considered still a baby. Seven was not such a young age.

The next day, and for many days after, I couldn't get the story of the different kind of people out of my thoughts. I wondered about them, where they came from, who they were, what circumstances had brought them to Lakota country. I also wondered why Grandfather had waited seven years to tell that story. Why had he told the story that night? Why then? It was like a secret he had been keeping.

2 The Others

Up until that moment, I'd never thought about there being any other world but the one I knew. Until then, I had thought my world was the only world. I'd look out across the prairie, or to the upper rise of the black hills, and think the world must end where my eyes could go no further.

Grandfather told many stories about the world, but it was always the world we knew. Again and again he'd tell us, "We are *Lakota Oyate*, the people."

I knew there were worlds beyond this one, the realms of the spirits and ancestors, but those were different realms. And I knew there were many other bands of people living on the land—we'd seen them, traded with them, sometimes married them and sometimes fought with them, but the Others that Grandfather described in his story were *a different kind of people*—that's what he said, like an owl is different from a sparrow.

All that autumn I drove *tanhansi* Rabbit crazy. When we weren't helping with the chores, I would drag him off to the edge of a clearing near a stand of pines and put him to work. We tried to recreate the shelter the Others had built. We cut small, smooth sticks from trees and peeled the bark, stacking them one atop the other until walls formed a space inside, a living space. My miniature shelter entertained the other children, and they began to add their own shelters to ours; a small camp grew. Grandfather sometimes walked by to watch us work. He'd shake his head, and then go off.

Rabbit and I even tried to duplicate the rolling cart. Grandfather told us it was called a "wagon." We didn't ask how he knew this word. In fact, I began to believe he knew more about these different kind of people than a single story could contain.

At night, I'd stare at stars above our tipi and wonder if the woman had her baby and had the baby lived? My mother and grandmother helped with the birthings in the village, and I knew sometimes the babies, or the mothers, didn't survive the birth. I thought of the man living in his log shelter all alone and decided no, he would leave if his wife didn't survive.

And was the baby, if it lived, a boy or girl?

I tried to ask my father questions about the camp of the Others, but he would not talk of it. He said it was time to leave childish curiosity behind and take on my training to be a hunter. I quit asking Father questions. Instead I bothered my mother and grandmother with endless questions about childbirth. They knew about healing, about plants—which could heal and which could kill—and I was suddenly interested in both. I began trailing along as they gathered the roots and leaves they would need for the winter.

During the buffalo hunt that fall, a young man of our village killed ten buffalo in one day. His name was Runs Fast. I watched the hunters bring in the buffalo and the sight amazed me. There would be abundant meat for the winter. I thought the name Runs Fast was a good name and I wanted to be such a hunter one day. We celebrated Runs Fast and his amazing hunt with three nights of feasting, and preparing the animals. The meat that was not being cooked was cut into strips and dried. Every night there were dances, music, and the smell of buffalo stew circling the air around the camp. The younger children spent entire days gathering young turnip roots and greens to prepare with the meat.

On the third night, I saw Runs Fast leave the light of the cooking fires and walk away. I followed him. When he'd cleared the camp boundary, I caught up with him and said, "You are a hero, Runs Fast."

He bent and picked up a small stone from the earth and tossed it out across the open meadow. "I am not a hero, Little Chief. I am a hunter."

"But everyone says you are a hero for killing ten buffalo."

Runs Fast laughed and said, "It is not hero's work, Little Chief, to do what is necessary for the people."

His words confused me. "But you are a wealthy man, to have so many buffalo robes."

Again he laughed, but he was not laughing at me. The birds asleep in the trees scattered and twittered when he laughed. "What is rich, Little Chief?" he asked. "I have one buffalo robe, like you. The others belong to my mother. She will give them away at the summer ceremonies."

"Give them all away?"

"Yes. I am only rich because of my mother. And father. A man is only rich when he gives away what he has no need of, what can be better used by others."

I had heard the boasting and bragging of many hunters much less accomplished than Runs Fast. His words amazed me, and that he would perform such a feat and give the robes away, or leave the celebration so others would not call him 'hero.'

"What is it like, Runs Fast? To kill a buffalo?"

He did not answer me for a long time. I looked at his arms and saw the strong muscles beneath his skin. "It is necessary, Little Chief. That is all," he said.

"Have you ever seen the Others that Grandfather speaks of?"

My question appeared to startle him. "The Others?"

"Yes, the people who are different from us, the people with white skin?"

"No, Little Chief. I hunt buffalo, not people."

Never once did I consider that Runs Fast's words had any importance beyond that moment. Not until many years later.

That winter, Rabbit finally got sick of hearing me talk about the Others. "What is the matter with you, Little Chief?" he asked. "You talk of nothing else. It's boring."

"What's boring? Don't you care that there may be a whole different kind of people out there with pale skin building things with logs? They may be dead. There may be others who have joined them. How can you say it's boring?"

Rabbit punched me in the shoulder. "Because it is. Boring. We are hunters. We are supposed to be learning to hunt. Instead you are like a squirrel hunting nuts—all these questions fill your cheeks and make them chubby."

Rabbit was only a little younger than I. We'd learned to walk together. He was my best friend and brother. After me, my mother had not born another child and I knew she wanted more babies. She was always doctoring with Grandmother, and sometimes I'd catch her watching some of the other young mothers holding babies with a sad look on her face. Once I heard my parents talking late in the night. Father said she was keeping me small, that it was time for me to train and not be hanging around the women all the time. Mother started to cry and Father quit talking harshly to her, pulled her into his arms and whispered to her, but the next day he took me from her fire. From then on, I spent my days with him and the other hunters.

Rabbit and I learned to make and use our first bows and arrows that winter. Until then, we had had only toys. The craft was painstaking, choosing the wood, peeling the bark back, stringing the sinew. The arrows were even more complicated, but we liked the activity and sat for hours hearing the men tell stories about hunting.

Our fathers no longer let us join the younger children in Grandfather's tipi every night, but took us into their circle. I liked being with the men, but I missed Grandfather's stories, although he'd never spoken again about the Others.

To be a great hunter was important for the survival of our people and the good ones were always remembered with tales of their feats. Grandfather often joined the hunter's circle. He'd bring out a single tooth, or bone, or horn that hunters had given him, and he'd use the object to tell a story about that hunter, that hunt.

On days so cold and crisp you could see your breath, Rabbit and I spent the hours beneath the bright sunlight learning to track small animals. I shocked everybody (myself included) by bringing down a small mule deer with my new bow. Much was made of my feat by Father and the other hunters and the animal was dressed, the hide scraped, and the meat fed to the whole village that night in a feast. Rabbit's father gave me a gift—a flute he'd cut from a thin stick of ash. The sides were carved with tiny animal figures and, although I did not yet know how to play it, I treasured the gift.

Later I walked beneath the brilliant stars and felt myself a man for the first time. It was a grand feeling, a feeling that almost faded my curiosity about the Others, at least for the time being. Something large had grown inside me and I could find no words to express it. Instead, even on cold days, I'd go to the edge of the village and play my flute, listening to the wind wail in the trees. It was the sounds of the world around me that I attempted to bring forth from the flute.

That winter the snow was deep. It drifted up around each tipi until we were warm and snug inside. I'd come out of the dim light of the tipi and the blazing blue of the sky would hurt my eyes, every twig of every tree glazed and glittering in the sun.

Spring came at last and we broke camp and began traveling south. I was always excited to see the tipis coming down and the people moving once again. Winter was quiet, a time for stories, for making songs, for tanning hides; spring was another thing entirely. I lived for spring each year.

After the encounter with Runs Fast—after killing my first deer—I was burning for manhood to arrive, impatient and in a hurry. I thought no more of the Others but spent my days in training. With Father's help, I built an even stronger bow than any I had yet held. The bow was stronger than my body, so I spent the days of spring pulling the sinew, stretching and stretching, holding it until my arms quivered and sweat broke out on my brow. Without ever notching an arrow, I held the bow taut. The younger children began teasing, calling me Little Tree, so long did I hold my stance. My arms grew strong, the muscles stringy and tight beneath my skin.

To make my lower body as strong as my arms and upper body, I ran. I ran up rocky hillsides, through the woods, down the stream. I'd race up the hill, gaining the meadow, and breaking fast into almost a gallop.

One day, after such exertions, Rabbit caught up with me and asked, "Little Chief, why are you in such a hurry to be a man? Everything has its time and manhood will arrive soon enough. Come, swim with me—or let's go fishing."

I stood, still holding the bow, when suddenly Rabbit's question pierced me like an arrow and I realized what I was doing. It shocked me. It was not manhood I sought—but the Others. I was training because I wanted to follow the trail my father and uncle had followed when they found the man and his pregnant woman; the Others. All of my training was for this purpose alone. I wanted to travel south to the steaming river. I wanted to go in search of the shelter of logs, of the man with a pale, hairy face, the woman and her large belly. I told Rabbit this.

"You're crazy, Little Chief. Those other people may not even be there any more. Likely they died, or left, or got eaten by a bear. You're crazy."

"I'm not."

"Sure you are."

I tackled my cousin and wrestled him to the ground. We were beside the river and Rabbit gained his feet, grabbed me by the ankle, and dragged me across the ground. Although I was older, and had been in fierce training, Rabbit was, like his name, quick and strong. He dragged me to the river and, before we knew what had happened, we'd rolled off the bank of the creek and into the water.

The frigid water closed in around us and we both leapt to our feet, sputtering and shivering and laughing. "You look like a drowned rabbit," I told my *tanhansi*.

He shoved me and I fell back into the water and we had a great water fight. The children heard the commotion and came running down to the riverbank. There was still snow on the tops of the mountains and the water was icy, but nobody cared. The little ones jumped in and joined our games, tagging one another and pushing each other down.

When I finally pulled myself out of the river, I saw Runs Fast standing on the edge of bank smiling at us. I felt like a child again. Rabbit was right; manhood would come in its own time.

Later, as we dried off, Rabbit pulled the braid out of his hair and said, "At least I got you to swim, crazy boy."

As the summer sizzled in, burning the grass and cracking the earth, Rabbit and I both reached our eighth year. Rather than getting me to play more, he went the other direction and began training with me. He was well named. He was lean, and quick, and nervous. I was more solidly built, with sturdy legs and a wider frame. We made a good team. Rather than totally abandoning youthful play, Rabbit convinced me that swimming, scaling trees, swinging from branches, and rock climbing were all equally good training to be a hunter. We were together day and night. Sometimes we'd gather the other boys together and stage great pony raids, knocking each other from our horses and snatching the leather reins from the losers. We also managed to get into some scrapes.

Rabbit and I often lost track of time and wandered far from camp, realizing too late that we could not return by mealtime. Once we convinced three of the younger children to eat a type of mushrooms we knew would give them the belly trots. Another time we rigged the trees in a small grove with small animal skins strung from branches on almost invisible lines of sinew. Rabbit convinced three of the girls our age that he had seen an entire flock of flying squirrels. He lured them into the grove where I was hiding—ready to make the flying pelts attack the younger girls.

After each of these escapades, we were confined to the village grounds, forced to do what Grandfather called 'woman's work' for three days. We were not even allowed to take our horses out for a ride during our restriction. After the incident with the girls, my mother doused both Rabbit and me with cold water, to get our brains working again, she said.

For the next two summers, we continued both in our training as hunters and as boys playing pranks. My mother finally carried a second child to full term (two others had left before gaining this world) and I had a baby brother. With this event, I felt one step closer to manhood. Something about the responsibility of being a big brother brought this home to me. I had a new place to hold in the family, now more man than boy, I decided. Mother spent her days in the care of the little one who was first named Shaking Leaf for the grove of aspens he'd been born under in the spring of the year.   Later my brother would be given a new name.

Had I known these easy years marked the end of my childhood, I may have cherished it more; the peaceful play, the easy rhythm of summer and winter in my village, the pranks Rabbit and I performed.   My parents were always watchful, always nearby, and Grandfather and my uncles were training us to step away from play and toward taking on our new roles as men.   The thoughts of the Others faded into the background of my life, not gone, but not haunting my every moment either.

Until the night the dream came to me.   And I caught it.

3 The White Bear Dream

The summer I reached my eleventh year, my little brother was toddling around with the other babies. I liked walking the woods to show him small anthills, a butterfly lighting on a bush, the birds flying above. Somehow, seeing the world through his eyes made it seem new and interesting again. It also made me feel more man than boy. Even my body was changing, my legs gaining length, my head now taller than Rabbit's by a hand. Mother teased me about having to cut new moccasins for each year. My feet were a man's feet.

That summer, just before the sun reached its highest point, we broke camp and moved again to the south to meet with other Lakota bands, family members and relatives, for the summer gathering. This time of gathering was my favorite. There would be great feasts, games, dances, and time for stories. I also knew, in the back of my mind, that the gathering place was nearer to the place where steam rose from the rivers.

The Others were on my mind again. Although I had managed to push the thoughts back the past two years, for some reason my curiosity about them was alive and hungry once again. I knew from Grandfather's story that the line of hills led south to the hot river, and the river led to the place of the Others.

When the new was camp set, and the relatives were gathering from great distances, I had the dream. It was a warm, sticky night and I slept on top of my buffalo robe to stay cool. Shaking Leaf snored in his small boy way, and both of my parents slept soundly. I drifted off to sleep in the soft surround of my parents' tipi and then, sometime in the middle of the night, I awoke and sat straight up in the dark.

The dream was so real, with sound and color, more like a place I had visited than a dream. For long hours after, I lay awake staring up and out at the tipi poles that seemed to reach for the stars themselves. Yes, I thought, this is a dream I should pay attention to, a dream I should talk to Grandfather about.

I moved through the next day as if asleep; so clear was the dream in my mind. It was as if I were still there—and not here. I told Rabbit about the dream, but no one else. More relatives arrived, but I scarcely saw them. Finally, I caught Grandfather Whirling Hand alone and said, "I had a dream. I need to tell you this dream later, when you have gone to your tipi."

He eyed me carefully and said, "Yes. Come and tell me your dream."

When all the feasting and dancing was done and the little ones tucked into robes for the night, and the cooking fires only glowing embers circled by the young men talking together, I left the village common area and went to his tipi. I dipped my head through the opening and said, "Grandfather?"

"Come in, Grandson," he called out to me.

I went in. Grandfather Whirling Hand sat alone in the dim light of the tipi, his back to the skins, his eyes watching the opening. He was holding a small horn, wrapping the end with sinew, his hands so familiar with the task that he had no need of good light. I circled the space and took a place beside him. The night was too warm for a fire and so only the last rays of daylight coming in through the tipi opening allowed us to see each other.

"What is it, *Takoja*?"

"I had a dream last night."

"Good. Tell me about this dream."

I stared at the cold fire pit a moment and said, "I was sound asleep and I heard a growling noise; it was loud and so near. The growling didn't seem like an attack sound, but hurt, as if something was hurting the animal. I went to see what was making this noise. And then along a creek I saw a big white bear, a grizzly I think, and it was growling."

"The bear was white?"

"Yes, Grandfather."

I knew the many stories surrounding the white buffalo calf, but I had never heard a story about a white bear. "The bear sounded like it was crying, Grandfather. I saw he was tied to a tree, the rope so tight around his neck that, when he struggled or moved, it cut into his fur. He was trying to get away. I went closer and saw his neck bleeding where the rope had cut him."

Grandfather listened, nodding for me to go on.

"I knew I could cut him loose but I didn't. I just watched him struggle. I felt bad for the bear." I reported every small detail of the dream. Grandfather said little, listening in the dimly lit tipi.

When I finished, he said, "*Takoja*, this is a strong dream for you. A sign. Someday you will come across something, or see something, that will be similar. It may not be a bear, but something else. When you see it, you will know and understand that it is related to this dream. And what you must do is set this white bear free. It will require something of you. Dreams such as these are never easy. That white bear wants freedom. You must grant it to him."

"I will know it when I see it?"

"Yes. You will know. You will see this in the future." He closed his eyes for a moment and said, "It is near. Wait. You will know." Grandfather looked at me for a long moment, as if considering something. "You are young to have such a dream."

"I am eleven winters, Grandfather, nearly a man now."

He smiled and I thought again of the night Grandfather had told me the story of the Others, the way his smile had made me think of lightning cracking a dark sky.

"Go now, Little Chief," Grandfather said. "I need to pray. You will know when you see this thing that has come into your dreaming. Dreams come from *Wakan Tanka,* from the Great Spirit."

When I left his tipi, the dream still surrounded me. I heard the low growl of pain and frustration, saw the white bear tied and bleeding, and sensed the purpose Grandfather had spoken of. I was to free this bear. My belly tightened and my back straightened as I thought about what he had said.

I'd had a dream, no—a vision. This vision contained something of my future. Boys do not get visions. Only men get visions. And Grandfather said to watch for this white bear, or something similar. I stood outside my parents' tipi for a long time. I walked behind it, away from camp to consider this dream. It was still warm outside but I shivered as if snow, and not sunshine, was on the wind. I rubbed my arms and went in search of Rabbit. I found my cousin sitting on a stone on the lower part of the slope behind the village whittling a piece of wood with his knife.

"I talked to Grandfather about my dream." I told him all that Grandfather had said.

He stopped whittling and looked up. "Will it be dangerous? This white bear?"

"I don't know. He didn't say, only that I would have to set him free when I found him."

Rabbit said, "But this white grizzly could kill you— pow—with one whack of its paw."

I shivered again, imagined cutting the rope from the growling white grizzly of my dreams. "It might. Kill me."

Rabbit picked up the small chunk of wood he was carving and showed it to me, an odd look on his face. "I am making this for you. For your pouch."

I took the small carving and looked. Emerging from the top of the pale wood was the head of a bear.

The council and ceremonies filled the village with activity. There were feasts and dancing and singing every night. All day the men met in the council tipi, going in and out, taking care of the business of the people, but I thought only of that white bear.

When would I see it? How would it be different? Should I be looking for it? The questions hounded me day and night until I caught my mother watching me—to see if I was sick or something. Rabbit finished the carving and I slid the small wooden figure into my pouch, feeling its added weight as if I'd filled the pouch with stones instead of one pale piece of fresh wood in the shape of a bear.

The village had grown to four times its normal size. Each band circled its tipis and there were six circles, the tipis dotting the valley for a great distance as we camped along the wide stream. More people continued to arrive. It had been three years since our separate family bands had gathered and all day long people called out to each other in greeting. The women gathered to admire the new babies born in the last year to cousins and sisters. New wives and husbands were introduced to family members, and wives and husbands were chosen for those who had not yet married.

My mother found her sister and cried out in joy when she saw her. Snow Woman had also had a baby, and both sisters were now mothers again and had much to talk about.

And there were quiet times; a time for tears and mourning for the old and the very young who had not survived the icy winter months.

Normally, this was my best time of the year, this gathering of old friends and relatives, and this year the gathering was especially large. Our single village expanded to several hundred people camped in the open expanse along the river.

But the dream had changed me. I was waiting, always waiting to see when the dream would arrive in my world. I watched the children's games and felt apart from them, no longer a child. I watched the feasting, the gathering of men, and felt not yet a part of their circle either, not yet fully a man.

On the third night of the gathering, after the ceremonies had ended for the evening and the women carried their children to the tipis to tuck them in for the night, I overheard the men talking about the Others. My uncle waved me over. I came and sat beside the men. It felt good to be included. I listened. The men who had traveled the farthest had many reports about the Others. They had seen them in the rolling wagons, crawling slowly across the land. Three of the men had approached them, trading with the strangers, or helping them fix a wagon wheel. Even as I heard the men speaking, my body shivered again, more violently this time.

This quivering in my body felt connected to my dream, to the white bear. It was also connected to any mention of the different kind of people who were coming. As I sat watching the fire, my knees hot from the crackling, burning wood, even my legs shivered. Grandfather had said the dream was *Wakan*, sacred. My uncle glanced at my face, at my jittering knees, and asked, "Are you okay, my boy? You are shaking."

"I'm fine, Uncle. It must be all the excitement. It jumped into my knees."

Uncle put his hand on my shaking knees and stilled them. That strong hand felt good and the quivering stopped.

That night the idea popped into my mind fully formed, and as real as the dream I'd had of the white bear. I moved through the next day like a chunk of wood until finally I pulled Rabbit away from the evening dances and games and took him to the edge of the camp.

"What is it, Little Chief?"

I shook my head, signaling silence, walking until we were out of earshot from any of the relatives. "I want to go see the Others, these different kind of people Grandfather talked about. I need to go."

"You're crazy, Little Chief. Why would you want to do that?"

"I think the Others are connected to my dream. I think I am supposed to go and see them."

"But it must be days and days away from here. You can't go alone—and nobody will take you. Grandfather said we moved north to stay clear of the Others." Rabbit whispered nervously, although there were no people close enough to hear us talking.

"I have to go." Even saying the words aloud felt right.

"We'll get in big trouble. How can we get away— without telling somebody?" asked Rabbit.

He may not have realized it, but I knew Rabbit had just agreed to go with me. "So you will go with me?"

"Sure I will. When we are old enough. When it is time." He punched my shoulder. "We have no strong horses. Think about it. We have only old horses, Little Chief, the horses that are too old for a hunter to ride. Grandfather says it is time for us to start learning to hunt buffalo, to learn to shoot our arrows, to become men. We should wait."

"I can't wait. It is all I think about. It will be one full year yet before we are allowed to hunt buffalo. You know that. Listen, you don't have to go. I can do this alone."

The desire to go find the Others had become more than a desire. It became a thing I must do. Just saying the words strengthened my feet on the earth. I felt it, like a snap in my body. I would go. I would take a horse, fill my pack, and go to see the Other people. "I'm going, Rabbit.

After I leave, you can tell my parents where I have gone so they won't worry."

Rabbit hissed under his breath. He walked ahead, turned and walked back, walked a circle around me, and then came to stand in front of me. "I will go with you, Little Chief. It is too dangerous for you to go alone. What if you get hurt, or snake bit? What if you take a fever, or the man with the wagon ties you up? No. You can't go alone."

Again I thought my cousin well named, jumping forward and back like a rabbit. I put my hand on his shoulder. "You are a good cousin, Rabbit. But I can do this. I don't want to get you into trouble."

"Shut up, Little Chief. I'm going with you."

"In the morning then," I said.

"So soon?"

"Yes. But we have to leave very early. The men rise long before the sun does. We'll have to be gone by then."

4 The First Journey South

Later, in the noise and jumble of the festivities, it was easy to fill packs with dried meat and fruits. It was easy to take two extra buffalo robes. We stashed everything behind a large pile of boulders near where the horses were tied.

It was too easy.

I should have been shivering now with fear, with going against my father and grandfather but since making the decision, the shivering had stopped. My body felt calm, my mind firm. I was not afraid. I wanted to tell my parents so they would not worry, but I knew we would be stopped if I said a word. And I was not going to be stopped from doing this thing. No, we have to go, and quietly, I thought. No one must know.

It was easy to arrange to sleep in Rabbit's tipi because my mother's sister and her new husband and baby were staying with my parents. Mother welcomed one less body in the already crowded tipi.

The night passed slowly, even more slowly once Rabbit and I pretended to sleep on our robes. For the longest time, I stared out at the stars winking in the night sky. I liked the way the poles reached like wooden fingers for those stars. I felt Rabbit beside me, as fully awake as I was. Outside, the encampment was quiet, the stillness of sleep settling over the people.

I reviewed my dream once more. It was strange the way I felt the rope around the White Bear's neck, as if it circled my own neck. I felt the pull and cut of it, felt the warm blood trickling down my own neck. The dream is *Wakan*, I reminded myself. Not to be feared.

Sleep. I willed my mind to quit rambling, willed my body to take its rest for the long journey ahead. My mind and body ignored my will. Finally, when all within the tipi were deeply asleep, I reached a hand over and nudged Rabbit. My cousin clearly had not had the same trouble sleeping as I had. He did not awaken but grumbled and curled back into his buffalo robe. I considered slipping out alone and taking this journey I must take without the company of my cousin, but I knew that would not be right. I nudged him harder until he woke up.

It was long before sunrise when we crept soundlessly out of the tipi and into the empty, open common area. We collected our packs and the hidden buffalo robes, tying them to our horses. We did not want to risk alerting anyone by riding the horses out of the village so we hushed them, walking far out and away before mounting. My plan was to go east until we cleared the foothills and reached the open prairie. Then we would follow the edge of hills until we were far enough south to find the hot stream. Grandfather had said two days ride to this place. I calculated that the summer camp must be about where the village had been when my father and uncle had seen the Others, before we moved north to stay clear of them.

Rabbit was quiet beside me and we rode without talking. The night was large around us. Never had we been out this early, or this far from camp. The stars seemed to press down from the heavens, and the darkness made my ears keen; I heard every sound the night contained. When we had ridden so long the sun was finally touching the dark sky, Rabbit's silence began to worry me. In spite of our utter aloneness on the land, I felt the need to whisper. "Rabbit?"

"Yes."

"How are you?"

He didn't answer right away. "I'm afraid, Little Chief."

"The animals sleep. Nobody followed us. There is nothing to fear."

"No, Little Chief. I am always afraid."

I listened to the soft clop of the horses' hooves on the dry grass and considered his words. They were almost a confession, a hum beneath the dark layer of sky. *Always afraid.* I knew what it must have cost my cousin to come with me on this journey. Rabbit was born afraid. His mother had died birthing him and I wondered if that was at the center of his fear. Being in the world had cost his mother much. "Thank you for coming with me, *tanhansi.*"

We rode on and on in silence now. I thought back to when we were small, the times I'd found Rabbit alone behind a tree, or hunkered behind a circle of stone, always alone. The other children had teased him, twitching their noses at him, calling him bunny, and baby. I'd always felt protective of Rabbit. Now, here he was riding across a dark prairie to protect me.

Once I'd asked Grandfather why he'd named me Little Chief. He'd said it was because my skin was loose. This had confused me. I remember pinching my upper arm and saying defensively, "My skin is not loose."

Grandfather laughed at me and said. "It is, my grandson. You leave your skin and crawl into other people's skin. You wear their skin as if it were your own. Always taking care of others, always feeling their sorrows and joys. It is a necessary thing for a good leader. That is why I gave you this name."

At the time, I didn't grasp Grandfather's words. Now, however, riding across the dark prairie, feeling the protection of the hills recede behind us, I understood. I felt Rabbit's deep fear, had felt it for a long time. It was not the fear of physical danger but something else, something in his spirit. It was the reason I'd taken my cousin as friend. I had lost my skin and wore another's.

The pale light creeping along the horizon at last was a relief. The sun would clear these heavy feelings, this fear and darkness, and the day would be a good day. I worried about my mother discovering me gone. I tried to send a prayer or a message to her across the glowing land not to worry, that we were well.

The sun crawled above the dark line of land and something inside of me burst along with the darkness. It was so brilliant, so golden, that sun. I thought of Grandfather's stories, of this sun rising and setting over the land for thousands of years, of our people witnessing and honoring the coming light, this unending and unchanging cycle of days, seasons, and the people moving across the vast land. I tried to express these thoughts to Rabbit. "Did you ever think how the sun will still rise and set even when we are no longer here?"

Rabbit too had shed the silence of the night with the rising sun. He laughed. "You say crazy things, Little Chief. That's why I go with you, really. I don't want to miss a single crazy thing you say."

"Dog."

"No. Rabbit. Come on. I'll race you to that out-cropping in the distance. The pointed one." And he kicked his heel against the side of his pony and lit out across the land. The light was strong enough we no longer needed to worry about the surefootedness of the horses.

By midmorning the sky above us loomed cloudy and cool and we rode hard, stopping only to eat or to water our horses when we came to a spring or stream. The land was dust dry, and water was hard to find. We had to sidetrack toward the streambeds where the trees and bushes were thick. We scanned the land behind us frequently, wondering if a search party had been sent out. The village must have discovered we were gone by now, but I saw nothing. No movement, no dust trails, no sign of life on the giant land. The endless waving grasses looked like the fur of a great animal as we crawled along its back.

I had no idea how far we had come, or how far we had yet to go. I felt small. Never had I been this far away from the shelter and protection of my village. Never had I felt this alone. Rather than being afraid, however, I felt exhilarated, led by my dream, a path cut by *Wakan Tanka*. Soon I would see the Others who had so occupied my thoughts the past few years. It never once occurred to me that the man and his family might be gone, the shelter of logs returned to dust once again. It never occurred to me, so sure was I that this had something to do with my dream, my vision.

Day passed into evening without incident. We knew our horses were no longer strong enough for hard riding over many days and so we rested them often, sometimes walking along beside them to stretch our legs and relieve them of our weight. When the light faded, we moved in toward the protection of the low hills. We found a grove of trees and made camp. We dared not light a fire. How close to the Others we were, or who may be following, was unknown so we sat together without comfort of flame or light.

The enormity of our action had begun to settle into me. Rabbit cut a small branch and whittled the green wood with his knife, saying nothing. The night hummed with the song of crickets, the frequent skittering of some small animal, the scent of dust and dry grass. My nose, my eyes, my mouth had taken on a new form, had become larger somehow, magnifying the simple into the great. I got up, rummaged near our camp, and found a thin stick and a hollow log from a nearby downed pine tree. I sat down again and began tap, tapping the log with the stick, humming and singing softly. I wanted to make a song for this moment, a song to express the feeling in my belly, of being alone, of being unprotected and wide open to the night. Words formed in my mind, and I hummed and then sang the words:

I have no ears, *Tunkasila*
Until you speak, *Tunkasila*.
I have no eyes, no eyes to see,
Until you look, *Tunkasila*.
My voice has no words but your words,
Hear my words, *Tunkasila*.
Hear my plea.

I found the voice of the song and sang it louder, repeating the verses until each word seemed plump and alive. Rabbit hummed, whittling his wood and finally singing along. In this way we passed the last dim hour of daylight, the song offering comfort in place of the warmth of a fire. And then, as if in unspoken agreement, we ended the song, unrolled our buffalo robes, and lay down beneath the blue-black night. I picked up my flute. I played the notes of the new song, committing it to memory, and then I laid back and stared out at the night.

Rabbit said, "That's a good song, Little Chief."

"Thanks."

"We traveled a great distance today."

"We did. Yes, we did." I drifted off to sleep thinking of those words. We had, indeed, traveled a great distance this day.

I dreamed of the white bear. As before, he was tied to a tree, the fur of his neck dark with dried blood. He growled pitifully and I heard my voice tell him I was on my way, that I would rescue him just as Grandfather had decreed. When I awoke, my neck hurt, as if the rope had been tied there instead of on the white bear. I heard an owl call, a second owl respond. I had seen a white owl once, but I had never seen a white bear.

I said nothing to Rabbit about my dream. It was still dark and we ate a little of the dried meat we had packed. The meat caught in my throat and I nearly choked. Rabbit thumped my back until my eyes bulged and I could breathe again. We watered the horses, mounted and rode.

34

Rabbit asked, "What will you do, Little Chief, if you find this white bear?"

"I don't know. Grandfather said when I found it I would free it."

"I bet Grandfather is not happy with us."

"No. Or our fathers."

Rabbit laughed. "We really did it this time. We will have to carry firewood and peel turnips until we are gray hairs."

"Are you sorry you came?" I asked him.

"Not yet." He chuckled and kicked his pony into a trot. "Ask me tomorrow."

5 The White Bear

We traveled the second day as we had the first, stopping frequently, saying little, eating little so the meager food supply we brought would not diminish too quickly. We rested the horses. We walked them. The line of hills began to curve west and we followed it, noting the increased growth of pine and aspen, the greater abundance of water, the thicker undergrowth of the nearby forests.

Late in the day, we found the hot stream and I knew we were close. I felt it in my belly. We listened for odd noises, unnatural noises, but heard nothing. We went as far as the little waterfall my Grandfather had described and made camp there. We considered going further but the sun had dropped behind the hills and darkness was fast arriving.

It was not too dark, however, to strip down and test the warmth of that steaming pool beneath the falls. It felt good to wash off the dust of our travels. The day had been hotter than the first day and we were not accustomed to full days on the back of a horse. The water soothed our sore backsides. Rabbit wanted to hunt small game but we didn't dare build a fire to cook a rabbit or bird. After dark, we lay on our robes listening to the wind whipping up above the trees. We watched the black of the clouded sky. I was still listening for strange sounds. Grandfather had said his father and uncle had first heard strange sounds—banging and clamoring. I heard nothing but frogs and crickets in their nightly song, and the wind. The sounds soothed me but I slept fitfully, wondering if tomorrow I would finally see these different people who had strayed into our world.

I was jerked out of my sleep early the next morning by the sound of boys at play, horses whinnying, a woman's voice calling, the sounds caught and carried by the wind. Rabbit was already awake and listening too. Excitement, and a bit of fear, burned low in my belly. It must be them, the Others.

Quietly we rolled our robes and tied the bedrolls to our horses so we would be prepared to leave in a hurry if necessary. The sounds were far off yet, so we walked our horses, following the creek. Steam rose off the water just as Father had told Grandfather it had. The sounds got closer and closer and still we walked the horses, not wanting to tether them too far away in case we needed to get away fast.

We reached a place where, across the stream, the land curved down and then up to a small rise leading to a clearing. Not wanting to make any sound, Rabbit and I used signs to communicate. We tethered our horses to a tree and, staying in the undergrowth, went closer. Still, we saw nothing so I pointed to a cottonwood tree. Rabbit nodded. We grabbed the lowest limbs and climbed into the tree near the edge of the creek. He was ahead of me. When he was high off the ground he gave a soft whistle, a birdcall, and I knew my cousin must have spotted something. I scrambled up beside him and looked out.

In the clearing was a small structure built of logs. It had a sloping roof and a stacked stone mound from which smoke was rising. To the east of the shelter a fence of rough logs enclosed four horses within it. When my father had first seen this sight, the people were newly arrived, the cabin not yet built. Now, there were multiple structures similar to the main home. It looked like a small village to me.

As we watched from our high perch in the cotton-wood, two boys about our age came running out from behind the cabin. Just as my father had reported, they were pale-skinned, but these were boys, two of them. "Look Rabbit," I whispered. "Twins."

The boys chasing across the yard were duplicates of one another. Both had the same facial features. They had yellow hair, and were clothed in the fabric Father had described. At first I saw only their sameness but, as I watched, I noticed also their differences. One boy looked strong and sure; the other walked with an awkward gait, his arms slightly askew from his body. He was slower too, and seemed to stumble along rather than running easily like his brother. They were the same, twins, but different from one another somehow.

It was early in the day. We sat in the tree watching the boys in the meadow below until the sun crept up higher in the sky. The stronger boy would playfully push the other one down and ride him as if he were a horse. Then they would roll in the grass together wrestling and tagging one another. Every once in awhile the awkward boy would stop and stare out across the land as if he'd forgotten what they had been doing.

Rabbit finally whispered, "We should go now. You have seen the Others and we can go now."

"No. Not yet. Where are their parents?"

Then, as if in answer to my question, the man who must be the father came out of the rougher structure off to the east of the cabin. He hollered at the boys and they stopped their play and came. The older man gestured, swinging a tool in his hands. The stronger boy took the tool and he and the weaker boy walked to where the horses were penned. A woman came out of the cabin, her arms filled with a bundle of wet cloth. She walked to a place where a rope had been strung between the cabin and one of the other buildings. She began hanging the wet things out to dry.

I watched. The stronger brother worked while the slower brother watched, squatting down on his haunches.

When he got up, the stronger brother gestured, pointing nervously and looking over at the father.

We understood none of what was being said, but suddenly the father strode over, looked at the awkward boy and began yelling. He appeared very angry. We watched, stunned, as the father took the boy's arm and yelled explosively, slapping him with the back of his hand and then dragging him toward the creek. The stronger brother called out and the woman came running, her washing left behind. She stood a moment at the corner of the cabin, then picked up her long skirts and ran toward the father, adding her voice to the sudden sounds piercing the quiet day.

Rabbit nearly lost his hold on the branch. "What is happening?"

"I don't know," I said. "I think the boy is in trouble." The shivering was back in my arms and legs. It was as if I felt where the father had taken the boy's arm, as if I could look down and see bruises appearing on my own arm. "Look, Rabbit, I think he wet himself."

The front of the boy's pants were dark. His face was contorted in fear and pain as the father took him by the shoulders and shook him, yelling into his face, then turned and stomped away toward the cabin. The boy crumbled to the ground and began crying. The mother and the other brother went to him and seemed to hush his crying, but they looked afraid. The woman helped the boy up. She took his arm and guided him toward the steaming creek. His gait had gotten even more awkward and the other brother hung back, watching, glancing toward the cabin where his father had gone.

When she got to the creek, she pointed to the water. The boy stripped his clothes off and stepped into the creek and began washing himself, swishing his clothes in the water.

Rabbit and I stared. The naked boy was pale as a white rabbit. I saw where the sun had baked his hands and face and arms brown, but everywhere else the flesh was pale. My stomach churned at the way the father had treated the boy. Something was not right. The stronger brother ran to the cabin and returned minutes later with other clothes. The woman gave the dry clothes to the boy. He dressed himself with jerky movements, still crying.

"Something is not right, here, Rabbit. Never have I seen such a thing." I wasn't sure if I was talking about the pale skin, the crying boy, the angry father, or my own uncanny response to all of these things.

"We should go now. Right now." Rabbit said.

"No."

"But what can we do? That is one angry man. I don't want him to see us."

"I said no. Wait."

The father emerged again from the cabin. He had a strip of leather in one hand and a rope in the other. He was muttering aloud. He reached the creek and began yelling again, now at the woman. She stepped back. So did the brother.

We watched in shock as the father took the rope, tied the boy to a tree, and then took the leather strap and began flailing him. He gave the boy maybe a dozen strokes of the strap. The mother and the other brother watched, no longer protesting. They had been silenced by the man's fierce anger. When the father finished whipping the boy, he turned, pushed the other brother and the woman away from the creek and they left, leaving the weeping boy tied to the tree.

The pale skin, the rope, the tree; all these images connected in my mind instantly. I was looking at the white bear of my dream. It nearly stopped my breathing as my thoughts collided with one another. I wanted to go to him but I was afraid. I could feel the boy's hurt. The punished boy cried into his hands, as if to hide his tears and anger. I felt the boy's anger, but it was a smothered thing, something that had been buried long ago. His smothered anger erupted in my own heart and spirit, and I wanted to march down, cross the creek, and rescue him. Just like that. "I'm going down there."

"What? Are you crazy, Little Chief? You can't go down there. They will see you. The father will come back and beat you. Or kill you."

"Then I will die. I have to free the boy. It is what I saw in my dream, Rabbit. Don't you understand?"

I descended the tree with Rabbit close behind. When we reached the ground, I headed toward where the boy was tied. It was upstream and we were still completely out of sight. The undergrowth was thick and there were many trees. I knew how to go quietly, to go unheard, and I did so now. Rabbit grabbed my arm and tried to pull me back but still I moved toward the boy.

When we were just a few paces downstream from him, Rabbit leaned and whispered into my ear. "You can't go to him. You will scare him half to death."

Oh, Rabbit was clever. He knew me so well. He realized the only way to cut off my intention to help was to suggest that my help could cause further harm. I stopped walking. I didn't want to cause additional fear or pain to the boy, and in truth, there was nothing I could do to rescue him at this time. I was only a boy myself. And we were alone, without the older hunters, without a strong enough bow—despite my boy's luck at bringing down the mule deer. I whispered. "You're right, Rabbit. I can't free him yet, but I do want to get closer, to see if he is all right. I won't let him see or hear me. You stay here, watch for any signs of the others. Warn me with your birdcall if you see anything."

I ran through the underbrush to a small bend in the stream beyond where the boy was tied. I stopped and smeared wet mud on my face and bare arms to better hide myself. I crossed the stream here and then inched my way toward the pale boy. I moved silently, with less noise than a squirrel, until I was directly behind a tree close to the one he was tethered to. My heart thumped in my chest but I kept my breathing quiet and steady so he would not hear me.

What I saw hurt me. The rope around his neck had opened up old scabs, just like the bear of my dreams, and blood trickled down his neck. I touched my own neck. I smelled the boy's fear. I smelled the anger and the hurt. I smelled the steaming water. My nose was ripe with all of these smells. The urge to step out from behind the tree, to rescue him, overpowered my common sense. I leaned my upper body around the tree and looked directly at him.

The boy was sitting and digging holes in the riverbank with his hands, as if he could bury his fear, and his anger, in those holes. His hands were muddy but he looked peaceful, like any ordinary boy at play along a riverbank, except for the rope. A small, crooked smile slid across his face, a sly look. He kept looking up and staring around him—as if he knew he was being watched.

Suddenly he caught my eyes staring at him. He leapt to his feet and screamed.

The sound of his scream jerked me back to reality. I knew that scream would bring the others—and danger. I darted behind trees and raced back across the creek and up the bank on the other side where Rabbit hid.

The boy screamed and hollered. I turned and saw the mother and the other brother come over the bank and race toward the yelling boy. He mumbled words to his mother but I could not understand them. It appeared she could not understand either—the boy was incoherent. The father came next, carrying a long, shining stick. The boy pointed and hollered and the man put the shining stick up in the air.

I was panting. So was Rabbit. We hid in the deep undergrowth and watched, too afraid to make a run for our horses.

The boy gestured, pointing to his eyes, crying. The father started yelling again. I thought it looked like the silly plays we'd put on when we were much younger, but this was no playacting. The father slapped the boy again, and the mother screamed at him.

Then the father raised the shining stick and we heard a loud crack. Fire shot from the end of the stick. The noise was so loud it raised the birds out of the trees, raised the hair on my arms. Terrified, we waited no longer. We ran as quickly as we could to our horses, walked them downstream until we were a safe distance from these Others, and then we mounted our horses and rode, never looking back, until we gained the higher, grassy ground where our tracks would be hard to follow.

Terrified the man would mount his own horse and follow us with his thunder stick, we rode until our horses were sweating and panting and could go no further. I reached a small thicket and rode into it with Rabbit close behind. I stopped and slid off my pony. My cousin still looked terrified.

"We can't push the horses any further," I said. "We'll take a different route home, stay in the foothills. It will take longer, but we will stay under cover that way."

Rabbit dismounted. "What was that stick? That man is a monster, a bad spirit. I'm scared, Little Chief."

"So am I. I'm sorry, Rabbit. I didn't mean to step out and let him see me. I was taken over by my craziness, my dream . . . that white bear."

"Keep walking, *tanhansi*. We can't stop."

It was slow going to stay in the hills instead of riding out onto the prairie, but neither of us wanted to risk being seen on the open prairie. That land was too naked. We stopped often to listen but heard no sounds of pursuit. We began to breathe easier.

"I didn't mean to scare him," I said. "Or you."

"Forget it. I think we're safe but we better keep moving." Rabbit laughed a shaky laugh. "I think it was not just that boy or me who was scared. You should have seen your face when you came crashing through the brush. When that thunder cracked."

"I nearly hit the ground. Something is not right there, Rabbit. That man is not a good man. I don't understand. There is much I don't understand. I wish I could go back."

Rabbit stopped. "You must be rabid. What do you mean you wish to go back?"

"Relax. I didn't mean now. But I will go back. I have to go back. That boy, the one tied to the tree, he is the white bear in my dream. I know it. And Grandfather said I must free him."

We marched ahead without speaking and then rode again until the horses were heated and panting. I walked back through my dream step by step a dozen times, a hundred times, reviewing each detail, wondering and wondering if I should have rescued the boy.

I needed to talk to Grandfather, to tell him what had happened. I wished we were walking into the village this moment so I could talk to Grandfather Whirling Hand.

6 The Race For Home

Our food supplies were getting low and we ate only a few pieces of dried meat and picked the raspberries we found in the open area of an old burn. As darkness approached, we were afraid to light a fire, afraid to signal our location to the man and his thunder stick. The moon rose and we lay on our buffalo robes and watched the sky. We heard an owl call. Sleep seemed elusive and distant and we talked.

"What are you thinking about?" I asked Rabbit.

"I was thinking about the hairy man."

I looked at my cousin. "You fool. Why are you thinking about that old scare story at a time like this?"

Rabbit laughed. "Don't know. I must like to be afraid. Remember how Grandfather used to tell us stories about that hairy man? He was big, very big, and would watch people when they didn't know he was there."

"That is just a baby story. Grandfather told that story to keep us from running too far away from the village; to scare us into our tipis before darkness came."

Rabbit ignored me and talked on. "The hairy man lived up north, where the lights play across the sky. The hairy man had supernatural powers, the power to make the lights dance across the sky. The power to steal your spirit out of your body."

I went up on one elbow and looked at my cousin. "A story, Rabbit, meant to scare small children. That's all. Go to sleep."

The night sounds—crickets, the wind in the trees, the frogs and buzz of mosquitoes—were familiar sounds, but failed to comfort me. Rabbit's breathing grew slow and regular, but my mind was full of all I had seen. Then, when the ease of sleep and dreams was about to take me, I heard an unnatural shriek. I jerked upright. Rabbit jumped up too and whispered, "What was that?"

"I don't know." I quickly reviewed all the animal sounds I'd ever heard. "That was not an animal."

"But it was not human either."

We sat, ears tuned to any and all sounds the night offered. I said, "It sounded far away."

Rabbit shook his head. "If we could hear it—it was too close for me."

Every sound in the forest, every rustle, every leaf turning seemed magnified. Rabbit said, "I think we should take turns sleeping. You rest and I'll listen. I'll wake you up when it is your turn."

I doubted whether I could get back to sleep. My skin tingled and my heart still pounded, all of my body was on alert. I lay back down and tried to slow my breathing but my mind still heard that terrible sound. When it cut the silence of the night a second time, Rabbit jumped beside me and said, "Let's go. I don't like this."

I felt like clobbering Rabbit for talking about hairy men and scary children's tales. It had made us both jumpy as babies, but we packed our robes onto our horses and began walking. It was still long before daylight and we moved slowly in the moonlight. The horses snorted and danced, acting strange and skittish. We didn't hear the shriek again, but were too nervous to stop except for brief rests periods. My stomach rumbled with hunger, and my fingertips tingled with fear. I sent a hundred prayers to *Tunkasila,* to keep us safe, to keep Rabbit safe.

I was sorry to have undertaken such a childish mission, sure now it would have been wiser to wait until we were properly trained. I hated to admit that I was still more boy than man, that I had endangered my loyal cousin, that I had stupidly stepped out from behind the tree and let the white boy see me. As we walked, I tried to focus only on getting safely back to the village, to my parents and Grandfather.

Whenever we stopped to rest, I thought I heard sounds behind us, sounds of someone—or something—coming. We walked and rode faster. When the daylight finally made riding easier, I told Rabbit I thought we were being followed. "Listen."

Rabbit cocked his ear to the wind but we heard nothing. Nothing. We mounted the horses and rode hard again for a time, and then walked them for an equal amount of time. In this way we passed the day, stopping only to water the horses and eat the last bits of dried buffalo meat. I knew our bows were sufficient to kill a bird or rabbit but we could not risk building a fire or stopping to cook a meal. Everything in me said danger was following us and we needed to keep moving.

I heard the noise of whatever followed every so often. We'd stop to listen, but when we stopped the sound would stop too. Once I heard heavy footfalls, like a horse, but two-footed. It had to be something big—and heavy. "Something comes," I said. "I can hear it. We have to ride."

We pushed the horses almost beyond their endurance, riding hard beneath a clouded sky. I was grateful the sun was not burning down on us. It made speed more possible. Finally, as the day again slid toward evening, we stopped and dismounted. "Rabbit, we cannot continue at this pace. We will kill the horses and this will be another bad thing on my spirit. How could I have allowed you to come? We have to slow our pace even if it means facing whatever is behind us."

Rabbit dismounted and looked behind us, taking a long, deep breath. He looked different to me, stronger, less afraid.

"Yes," said Rabbit. "We can't keep running. It isn't the way. We will put our trust and protection in the hands of *Tunkasila*."

Pride in my cousin filled me. I took my pony's reins and began softly singing the song that had been given to me during our journey south.

> I have no ears, *Tunkasila*
> Until you speak, *Tunkasila*.
> I have no eyes, no eyes to see,
> Until you look, *Tunkasila*.
> My voice has no words but your words,
> Hear my words, *Tunkasila*.
> Hear my plea.

I sang the verse a second time and a new verse came.

> Bring us safely home, *Tunkasila*,
> And we will walk for you,
> Hear our plea, we are calling for you.

Rabbit added his voice to the song and we walked, rode, and sang until darkness came once again. We heard pounding footfalls in the distance but they seemed to come no closer, or would disappear completely when we rested. The fear did not leave us, but the song tamed it.

That night we rested only during the darkest hours and, when the horizon lightened, we moved once more across the land. We stayed in the forest of the low foothills instead of out on the open prairie. We felt safer, but the path slowed us down. I was sure we would arrive at the village before dark. Thank you, *Tunkasila,* I whispered aloud again and again.

By midday we had been traveling for almost two full nights and days. I was weak with hunger and tired to my bones. I knew Rabbit must be equally tired. "How is your horse?"

"Tired. Like me. We are close. My horse told me this."

I laughed. "Good you can talk to your horse."

"What do you think has been following us? I hear two strong footfalls, then man, then horses, then no horses. I don't get it."

"I don't either. I sense it could have caught up with us—but didn't. I think we are safe. Look, there is Coyote Point."

Coyote Point was a stone outcropping shaped like the snout of a coyote. It pointed straight to our village. We mounted our horses and rode as fast as we dared toward home. Relief washed over me like cool water. I'd not realized how tightly I'd been holding my body since the moment I spied the Others for the first time. My muscles felt watery and weak now, but I also felt braver. "We should just stop and wait for whatever is behind to catch us."

Rabbit shook his head. "Your bravery comes mysteriously in sight of our camp. Ride, you foolish boy, ride."

My cousin knew me too well. I laughed and said, "I guess so. It is easy to feel brave now that the village is over that rise."

As we cleared the open meadow leading toward the camp, one of our uncles rode toward us. He was angry. "Where have you been? Everybody in the village has been searching for you."

Rabbit suddenly looked afraid once again. "Something has been chasing us."

"Never mind," the uncle said, but his anger seemed to evaporate and he grinned at us. "Get off those poor, sick horses. I will tend them. You boys get to the village."

We got down off the horses, handed the reins to our uncle, and ran to the camp. No sooner had we entered when Uncle followed leading our horses—with eight other riders behind him.

I couldn't believe it. My father, Rabbit's father, and several of our older uncles and cousins rode into the camp laughing and slapping each other on the shoulders. I understood and was ashamed.

Rabbit said, "They were behind us."

I nodded. "The whole way."

"That's what we heard?"

"Yes."

"Why didn't they show themselves?"

I knew why. "They wanted to teach us a lesson by scaring the breeches off us."

All the people came out to meet them, including Grandfather. I went directly to him and said, "I am sorry I left the village and took my cousin with me. It was wrong."

Grandfather looked stern. "You should have told someone."

"I know."

He looked at both of us. "Go to your tipis now. We will talk about this and determine your punishment."

Father stepped out of the crowd and came to my side. "You have caused your mother great worry."

"Yes, Father."

Grandfather put his hand on my father's arm and said, "We will talk about this later. Your boy has a story to tell us—and I have one of my own."

Father nodded and said "Go now."

7 *Maza*—Metal

The last thing I wanted to do was walk through our village. Rabbit stayed beside me, staring straight ahead. Behind us, our older cousins were already laughing and joking about keeping us on the run through two nights. When I turned and looked, my cousin, Walks With Horses, was showing the children how he had muffled the back hooves of his horse with boots of fur to create that strong, pounding two-footed sound.

I felt foolish and humiliated to know that, while Rabbit and I ran frightened day and night, eight strong hunters galloped behind us—protecting us. We deserved to be punished and humiliated for making the whole village worry, but knowing that didn't make the teasing any easier.

Mother faced me, a fierce look in her eye. All the while she cooked, she scowled, shaking her head and wagging a finger at me. Still, she cooked my favorite chokecherry *wojapi*, heating it over hot rocks in the cooking fire. She was both punishing me, and welcoming me home.

My mother's given name was Morning Star, to honor the moment of her birth. I thought it was the most beautiful name of any of the women in the village. However, on this day, it was as if the morning star had become a hot spark in her eyes. They flashed in anger, and perhaps relief, that I was safely home again.

To apologize for my actions, I brought armfuls of wood for her fire. I carried water and watched my little brother so she could go visit with her sister for a while. Doing these extra chores, however, no longer felt like punishment. The journey had changed me somehow. I felt older, stronger; the image of the boy tied to a tree had lodged itself in my head and wouldn't let go. Finally, when the evening meal was nearly ready and mother had returned and was feeding Shaking Leaf, I went in search of Grandfather. I found him sitting at the center fire with the men. He was eating.

"Grandfather, after you have eaten, can we talk? I have to tell you about what happened, and about my dream."

He said, "Come to my tipi when the sun goes down."

A meal had never tasted so good. I hardly kept from groaning as I ate the buffalo stew; I couldn't remember ever being this hungry. The journey had whetted my appetite for Mother's wonderful cooking, and I thanked her over and over until she finally smiled at me again.

Father's anger was not so easily appeased. After supper he took me aside, and in a firm voice, confined me to the village for four days doing work for the women.

I did not protest.

"Go then. Your Grandfather wants to see you."

Father's anger pierced me, but I couldn't find the words to explain the powerful reasons why I had done what I had done. It was not a prank, not my intention to make my family sick with worry—it was the dream. I had found my white bear. But none of these words came, so I nodded and left my family sitting by the fire finishing their meal.

"Grandfather, may I come in?"

"Yes, *Takoja*. Come in."

When I sat, he said, "Tell me what you saw, what happened."

I told him of the journey and, in greater detail, about what we saw the different kind of people doing. I talked about the two boys who looked alike, about the one who was awkward and slow, and how the angry father had whipped the boy for wetting himself and then tied him to the tree. I ended my story by admitting I had shown myself—and how the boy screamed with fear. "I was foolish, Grandfather, for doing that. But that boy, the one tied to the tree, he is the white bear of my dream."

He said, "You shouldn't have gone, Little Chief."

"I know this, Grandfather. But I had to. Rabbit tried to talk me out of it. It was not his fault. It was my fault. I don't want him blamed or punished for this. It belongs to me. I want the punishment to be mine alone."

He considered my words, holding his silence for a long time. "You should not have done this yet, Little Chief. You are still too young."

I straightened up, "I am not too young."

Grandfather shot me a stern look. "Did you free this white bear?"

"No."

"Why not?"

I was like a leaf curling in the heat of his stare. It hurt to say the words, but I had to utter them. "Because I am too young."

He seemed to relax. "You are not to return, not until you have learned to be a good hunter, to ride a stronger horse, to protect yourself and those who are with you."

Grandfather Whirling Hand's disapproval was much harder to bear than the teasing of small children. "Yes, Grandfather. There is something else . . . ."

"Yes?"

It was difficult, but I needed to tell him also about the shining stick that shot fire and thunder. I repeated each detail of our hasty retreat, our great fear of such an unnatural noise. "What was it, Grandfather?"

His response was low and slow. "This . . . this is what you have to be careful of, Grandson. It is some kind of *maza wakan,* powerful metal." The old man leaned to his left, pulled a leather bag into his lap, and dug into it. He took out a small, round object and handed it to me.

I examined it; round and hard like a stone, but perfectly smooth, and heavy. "Grandfather?"

"It is what comes from that thunder stick. This ball was taken from the body of my brother after the hunters he rode with encountered a band of the strangers wearing blue coats. They all had thunder sticks and this is what killed him. Stay away from this, Grandson. Never go back."

The now familiar shiver trembled through my body, the shiver I attributed to the dream of the white bear, to the boy tied to the tree, to a bloody rope, and my own need to free that boy. The words caught in my throat. "I can't promise that, Grandfather. I can't stay away."

"What are you saying, Grandson?"

"Grandfather, you said my dream came from *Wakan Tanka*. You said we must listen to our dreams, listen to those things that we must do. In my dream, I knew I was supposed to free this white bear, to remove the bloody rope and cut him loose. How can I do this unless I go back?"

"Ah, Little Chief. This *maza* is a bad thing."

The silence in the tipi grew heavy. I said nothing, but my back straightened again. But it was not stubbornness that straightened my spine—it was my dream.

He finally broke the silence with a sigh, and these words. "It is so, Little Chief. We must act on such a dream. How can we not? I will think on this, Grandson, but promise you will not return until I give you permission, until your training is complete, and you have a strong bow and a strong horse beneath you. You must give me your word on this."

"I give you my word, Grandfather."

"Here, keep this ball to remind you. Put it in your pouch, and take it out when the desire to return comes to you. Think of my brother being killed by such a ball. You must wait for the right time. Go now."

I put the ball in the pouch at my hip, but I did not get up to go.

"Now what is it, Grandson?"

"There is something else."

Grandfather gave me a weary smile. He had often said my curiosity made him lose sleep.

"I do not think I should be punished for acting on my dream. You said we must act when given a dream by *Wakan Tanka*. I only acted on my dream." I feared angering my Grandfather, but feared worse not speaking out and offering some defense for my actions. I dropped my head and waited. He said nothing. Finally I looked up to see him smiling at me.

"I accept your plea, Little Chief. You have argued well. Here then is what must be done. You have upset the *Oyate* with your runaway journey. They searched and worried. Your mother cried. Your father and seven others left the village to follow you. All of this has consequences. It is not a small thing you have done. To honor their care for you, and their tears and worry, your father and uncle, Rabbit's father, must hunt and kill an elk or buffalo to feed the village as payment for your action. Tomorrow they will hunt. And you and Rabbit will help the women prepare the cooking fires; carry wood and water to help prepare the feast." He paused and then added, "And we will have dancing and singing to celebrate. That is the right thing for you. Now go."

Grandfather's words overwhelmed me. He had found a way to turn my foolish actions into something to be both punished—and honored. This, more than anything else, humbled me. I was deeply ashamed for having risked my cousin, worried my parents, and even endangered my people by pulling eight hunters away. "I will do as you say, Grandfather. I will wait until I am stronger. And thank you."

As I rose to leave he said, "And I will tell your father, and Rabbit's father, to begin training you boys, to find stronger horses and stronger bows, to make you ready. It is time. Tell your parents to come and speak with me."

I left, the urge to leap and yowl like a wild dog strong inside of me. I had stood strong, acted like a man. It felt good. And I was to begin training, to get a stronger horse, to become a hunter. My feet were light as I walked back to my parents' tipi to get the rest my body cried out for.

Instead of returning to the tipi, however, I passed it and climbed the hill above the village. I looked out at the sky above, and saw the tipis below; the small fires burning within gave them a mysterious shine in the dark night. I thanked *Wakan Tanka,* my ancestors, and the spirits for our safe return to our families. This simple act, of giving thanks, made tears jump into my eyes. My dream had come from *Wakan Tanka.* I had come from *Wakan Tanka.* There was nothing else to say. I went down the hill to my mother and father and told them Grandfather Whirling Hand wanted to speak with them.

When my parents returned, it was late. Shaking Leaf was long asleep. They were no longer angry but looked at me with curiosity. My father's name was Charging Bull. Grandfather had given him that name when he avoided being killed by a bull buffalo as a young man. On this night, however, father's normally strong hands, his keen eyes, his voice all seemed softer, charged with deep feelings for me, his son. Again, I was overwhelmed that such a foolish act had brought so many changes.

Father said, "Tomorrow, my brother and I hunt for an elk or a buffalo. You will stay and help to prepare the fires, do as your mother asks. You will not leave the camp again, Little Chief. Is that clear?"

"Yes, Father."

He touched my arm. It was just a touch but I felt it clear to my feet. It both strengthened me—and reminded me that I was a boy still.

My exhausted body sought sleep, but my mind whirled and whirled with the events of the past few days. Finally, when it was quite dark outside, and both of my parents slept deeply, I again left the tipi and crossed the camp to Grandfather's tipi. With my voice barely a whisper, I called to him through the flap. "Grandfather, may I speak to you again?"

There was a long silence. I was about to leave when he called out softly, "Come in, my grandson."

He was stretched out on his buffalo robe, ready for sleep. He lived alone in his tipi; my grandmother had died many years earlier. He said his age and place had earned him this solitude.

When I came in, he said, "Sit."

I wasted no time. "When, Grandfather? When can I go back? How old must I be?"

"Why do you ask me this? Have I not said when you have a stronger horse, when you have a stronger bow, when you have learned to hunt the buffalo?"

"Yes, Grandfather. But I feel this white bear in my heart. He is hurting. I feel him trying to be strong like his brother, the one who looks like him, but he is not strong. I want to free him."

Grandfather rolled to his side and looked me straight in the face. There was a small fire burning; it cast a shadow, deepening the lines of his face and adding to his great age. "You must trust me, Grandson. I also have had dreams— dreams I will soon tell to the people. I feel your hurt, and through you, the white bear's hurt." He smiled gently, "I too have loose skin. But you must be a good hunter before you can go or you will endanger the boy, yourself, and perhaps your people. Now go. I am an old man. I need my sleep."

"Yes, Grandfather."

Once again I paced across the dark area between tipis. The fires had burned down to glowing embers and I sat down near the one in front of our tipi. I stared at the yellow, orange-blue glow of the near-dead fire and wondered about Grandfather's dreams. What did he see? How had dreams guided his life? I crawled into the tipi, pulled my robe outside, and laid it next to the fire. I stretched out on my back.

It was as if even the confinement of the tipi was more than my spirit could tolerate. I needed to be out here beneath the big, black sky, to see the stars winking down at me, to see the seven star boys who had climbed the heavens and made a permanent home there, forever to look down on us, their relatives. Grandfather had told us this and many other star stories. Finally, my spirit had drunk its fill of bigness, and I fell into a deep, dreamless sleep.

8 *Wocekiya*—Blessings

I awoke when the birds first stirred and began their singing. My parents still slept within the tipi. I sat up and took a long breath of the cool, moist air.

Today I am a man, I thought, and then wondered where such a thought had come from. I wasted no time but began scanning the underbrush near the village in search of dry, downed wood for the cooking fires. While I worked, I heard my father and uncle and three others ride out of the village. I knew they went to hunt, that my mother was now up and preparing to feed the entire village.

All day I worked carrying water, gathering the greens and roots my mother asked for, stacking yet more wood for the greedy fires. Rabbit joined me and we said little, working side by side for most of the day. I was pleased his punishment did not extend beyond this day's work. It had not been his fault. Once, after we had eaten our noon meal, I patted his shoulder and said, "Thank you for coming with me."

Rabbit said, "You could not have stopped me." He laughed and went back to work.

When the woodpiles were stacked as high as a small tree, and the fires were banked and waiting for the return of the hunters, I stopped working. The women sat near the fire talking and playing with their little ones. I went to the river and swam, cleansing my body of the sweat of the day. Then I washed my hair with yucca root and scrubbed my

scalp until it hurt.   It felt as if I was preparing for
a ceremony.   I spoke to no one after bathing in the stream,
but again climbed the hillside above the village and found a
granite boulder to sit on.   Below, in clear view, I saw all the
activities of the people.   I watched them play, talk, sew,
grind meal, feed their babies.   I watched the boys pitch
stones, and the little girls giggle at the boys pitching stones.
It was a peaceful scene, one I had enjoyed many times
before, but on this day it looked different.

I couldn't get White Bear out of my mind.   I suddenly
realized I had named him.   *Mato Ska*—White Bear.   That
meant the pale boy was now real in the world . . . in my
world.

What is it that makes White Bear slow and awkward, I
wondered?   His brother had clearly been born strong and
straight, but there was something not right about Mato Ska.
I knew there had been children like that in other bands of
our people.   I'd seen them.   They were considered gifts
from the spirits, these children.   There had also been twins,
although rarely.   These white boys were twins of the body
but, perhaps, not of the spirit.

Never had I seen a child whipped and tied to a tree, left
there to struggle until he bled.   Just remembering that sight
caused me to feel the boy's hurt again.

I thought about an older boy in our village who was
different.   He did not play or learn to hunt and ride like the
other boys.   Most days he sat at the opening of his parents'
tipi and drew pictures in the dirt with a stick, as if making
plans or something.   I often watched him, wondering why
he was not like other boys his age.   He liked to eat, rarely
left his spot near the tipi opening, and was mostly quiet.

I thought how, among my people, nobody attacks the
weak ones.   Only the strong ones are teased.   I had never
realized this before.   The elders approved of most games,
even games of trickery and the rougher games of riding
against each other with burning sticks and knocking each
other off our horses.   No, elders approved of the games,

but only if the games made us more quick and clever—never if the game attacked a person's weaknesses. Even the teasing Rabbit and I had endured the day before was aimed at us, not because we had been weak and foolish, but because we had been daring. And stupid.

Yes, stupid. There was also that.

The image of that father beating his son stirred something inside of me. I caught myself watching the people of my village. We were generally peaceful. Occasionally some violence erupted, usually between a man and his woman, but the Elders dealt harshly with those who did needless violence against another. It was not accepted. And I knew the hunters rode against other bands of people for horses, to settle a dispute, or to protect our territories, but that was simply our way.

Once I had seen a young hunter abuse his horse. The Elders punished him severely. He'd been forced to leave the village for one full moon, to live alone out on the prairie without his people or his horse. Another time I'd seen a man treat his wife badly—he had slapped her and pushed her against a tree. She and the other women, supported by the grandmother and grandfathers, had taken the man's belongings to the edge of the village and left them there. No one spoke to him for many weeks—and his wife took a new husband.

But this was not cruelty—it was justice.

From my perch on the hillside, I watched the people. Two young men walked their horses to the river and rubbed them down, laughing and talking as they did so. Children played games in the dirt with small sticks and stones. The women, as always, banded together to talk, care for their babies, cook the meals. The scene was one of peaceful camp life—so unlike the angry father and White Bear.

Grandfather's stories were always stories about justice and loyalty, about learning to be strong without being cruel. I had never realized this before, but the stories were part of our training as boys. The grandmothers told similar stories to the girls.

I wanted to understand my dream. Why had it come to me? Why was Mato Ska's father cruel to him? I wanted to free him but Grandfather said no, not until I had a stronger horse, and a stronger bow, not until I had learned to hunt the buffalo with the older men. Then I could do what *Wakan Tanka* had directed me to do.

No, there was nothing I could do for Mato Ska except pray to *Wakan Tanka* for his safekeeping, to protect him until the time came when I could free him. I sent my prayers out, concentrating hard on the boy tied to the tree. At last I turned my gaze to the village below.

As I watched from high on my stone, I saw the riders coming in from the west. My father, Charging Bull, and the other hunters returned. I saw they had killed an elk, quartered it, and split it between the horses. As they splashed across the creek, some of the children and women ran to meet them, laughing and calling out their congratulations on a good hunt.

There would be much work to do to prepare the meat for the meal. All thoughts of Mato Ska slid from my mind as I hurried down the hill to let my mother know the men were back.

With the return of the hunters, the peaceful camp erupted with bustling activity. I helped unpack the horses and carry the quartered elk to the preparation area. The women began scraping, washing and cutting, preparing the meat for the cooking fires. The older girls and elder aunties came and carried away the babies and young children to entertain them with stories and songs so the women could work.

As I watched the buzz of activity, I realized that the stories, the songs, the activities planned by the Elders—everything had a purpose. As a child, I'd thought it was just play. Now I saw how the mothers and fathers, the elders, all were focused on giving the young ones new skills and guidance toward the day when they would become mothers and fathers. The stories were not just stories; they were lessons.

When the sun began to climb down toward the horizon once again, the camp was filled with the scent of roasting meat, the hum of women singing and talking, the endless play of the children. My parents, Charging Bull and Morning Star, and Rabbit's relatives did as Grandfather had directed; they fed the entire village that evening. When the meal was ready to eat, Grandfather came from his tipi and spoke to the circle of people gathered. He waved at me and pointed to a space beside him.

He stood and said, "This feast has been prepared for us because your young cousin here," he indicated me, "was gone for several days from our village with your cousin Rabbit. Many of you searched for them, worried for them, and for this their parents offer you this food."

He did not talk about the dream or why I had left the village. When he finished speaking, Walks With Horses (one of the eight riders who had followed us) asked to speak. He told, in great detail, how they had located and followed us. Once again, he told how he had covered two of his horse's hooves with fur and leather to muffle the sound. Walks With Horses acted out the big hairy man descending on small children until all the people were laughing. Soon the older children were making faces at each other and giggling about the big hairy man.

I didn't mind the playful teasing. I thought back to the fear Rabbit and I had felt and realized again that the men running behind had only two things in mind—to see to our safe return and to teach us a lesson.

Then Grandfather said he would now do *wocekiya*, give blessings on the food, and we would eat. He prepared a small amount of food for the ancestors and spirits and prayed over the offering. Tears collected in my eyes as I thought of *Wakan Tanka*, of my father killing the elk to pay for my action, and that meat now being offered back up to the spirits to feed them. All was a cycle, it seemed, of giving and taking, of those living and those dying, and this fact touched my heart.

The evening passed in a noisy blur, the meal followed by drumming, and singing, and dancing. The children continued teasing me but I also saw that they now looked up to me. I had gone on a journey—and returned a changed person.

When the festivities ended, Grandfather spoke. "Tomorrow morning I want to talk to all of my people. It is time for some of these boys to gain stronger horses, to build stronger bows, to learn to hunt the buffalo. There is a herd of wild horses—many of you have seen them—led by a strong stallion, a fearless horse that no one has managed to catch. Go to sleep now and tomorrow our strongest hunters will find the herd and then capture and train them. I will follow with the boys who will ride the new horses home."

I curled into my sleeping robe filled with excitement. I hadn't expected our training to begin so soon. A horse. A strong horse. Grandfather had said that was the first thing I needed in order to complete what *Wakan Tanka* had told me to do in the dream. And it was happening now. I forced my eyes to close, my mind to quiet. A stronger horse required a well-rested rider.

9 Wasaka—The Strong One

Early the next morning, Grandfather chose the seven boys who were to go along, those who were to get the stronger horses. Rabbit and I were among the boys chosen. Grandfather explained that the hunters had already ridden out and that we would follow. He told us to get our horses quickly—it was time to ride.

On our way out of the village we passed the scout on lookout, the same uncle we had met when we returned to the village after our journey. He raised an arm and pointed in the direction that the hunters had gone earlier.

As we trotted along beside Grandfather he said, "From here on, you listen and follow my directions and the directions of the other hunters. Clear your ears and listen."

On the ride, Grandfather Whirling Hand pointed out the signs of the earlier riders, explaining all he knew about tracking and reading a trail. We listened to every word. Near midday, when the sun was high in the sky, Grandfather pointed to a ridge and said, "We will ride up to that ridge. I can see other tracks now. The hunters have found the herd of wild horses."

It is difficult to describe the feeling I had when we gained the top of the ridge, looked down into the shallow bowl below, and saw the herd of forty or fifty wild horses. It was like the sinew on my bow, stretching tight, and tighter still—that's how my body felt.

Grandfather pointed out the giant white stallion. "That horse is crazy. He will do anything to protect his herd. Watch now. Our men will cut some horses out," he laughed, "if they can get around that one."

We watched. The nine hunters scattered and broke into three groups. They surrounded the herd and closed in on it. I saw my father to the north of the herd. Rabbit rode up beside me, stopped, and said, "Have you ever seen anything like that?"

"No," I said. There were no words to express it. Those animals were huge and strong. They seemed to own this land and knew it. Our riders looked small as ants by comparison.

Grandfather laughed as the riders forced the white stallion to race up a steep incline, the herd following him. "That horse is smart, fearless—and crazy," he said again.

The men worked the herd expertly, cornering here, chasing there until they came together like dancers and cut eight or nine horses out of the herd. One of my uncles was holding four of our trained horses and, as soon as the others had cut the herd, my uncle moved in and took the lead with the four tied horses. They immediately began to lead the nine horses that had been cut. It was so smooth, so flawless and thrilling, that I gave a whoop and punched my fist in the air. I counted. There were thirteen horses; nine wild, four trained.

Charging Bull and the other men drove the horses fast, heading east toward our village. We younger boys followed at a distance with Grandfather.

Near the village, the men had already prepared a natural enclosure of stone and hillside and downed trees for the animals. It was a spacious corral with no easy escape. The men drove the wild horses into the enclosure, jumped down from their own horses, and quickly tugged dead trees across the opening.

Over the next four days, we camped with the men to watch the training of the nine horses. Grandfather explained that the wild horses would get no food or water until they took it from the men. The men would enter the corral making the huffing sound of a horse. They offered food and water and the trained horses came easily. The wild horses shied and stayed distant. The men said nothing, just stroked and rubbed the noses of the trained horses.

Grandfather explained how the men had no need of words, that horses could read a man's intention—even understand his thoughts. Horses were uncanny like that, he said. They were able to sense the slightest fear in a man— or the slightest violence—and so the men remained calm and quiet, offering food and water again and again throughout the day.

When we were not working with horses, my father and uncles helped us to build yet stronger bows and arrows. They showed us how to pull the bow taut and hold it, to aim and shoot. We slept beneath the stars and the older girls brought meals out to us. We did not return to the village but stayed with the men, sleeping out beneath the black sky, listening to the sound of the horses stamping and whinnying.

The horse camp so absorbed my attention, I scarcely thought of Mato Ska. As each day passed, the wild horses were tamed by their own thirst and hunger—and by the example of the other trained horses. One by one, although they trembled and snorted and shook, the wild horses began to approach my uncles, accepting water and allowing them to touch their noses. The men remained calm and fearless at all times, completely aware of each horse, sending them silent messages that they would not harm them. I was fascinated.

During the third day of watching the men train the horses with patience and calm, with steady gentle effort, it occurred to me that when I had stepped out from behind the tree and frightened the white boy, I'd done it all wrong. That was why he screamed and screamed. That white boy was like these wild horses, caught in his own world of fear and trembling.

When the men finally took braided sinew and soft leather and put the wild horses on a rein, careful to make sure it did not hurt their mouths, I remembered the bloody rope tied to White Bear's neck, and the whip the boy's father had used. No wonder he wets himself, I thought.

On the fourth day, my father said they would ride the wild horses. My heart raced. I'd become completely absorbed in the training—and in the horses themselves. I felt their fear, their confinement, and their restless spirits. I felt their thirst and hunger, and their need to do what felt undoable.

Charging Bull and the other men got on the trained horses and rode them around the enclosure. When all were moving in the same direction, he called out to the men standing at the tree blocking the entrance to pull the tree away. They rode their horses out and the wild horses followed. I resisted the urge to holler and cry out, realizing the wild ones could still become frightened.

We ran to watch as the men rode the whole herd straight into the deepest part of the river. Again the riders remained silent, but what unfolded was a sight I had never seen.

The river became a churning storm of men and horseflesh. The men slid off the tame horses into the water and touched the trained horses first. Then they moved and touched the wild ones. They swam with them, stroking, rubbing, and moving from tame horse to wild horse in a kind of wet confusion. I felt as if I was in the water with them—both boy and horse. The water allowed the wild horses to adjust to the feel of a rider on their backs for the first time. Finally, Charging Bull signaled the riders and, in a great splashing, wet exit, they came out of the river and rode hard off to the south across the open prairie.

Only when they were gone did we let our excitement reach our mouths. We hollered and laughed and cheered.

The blood was singing in my body. I couldn't contain myself and dove into the river. The others followed me.

The men rode the horses to exhaustion, finally circling back and returned to the training camp. I saw the men were excited but tired, too. The wild horses were panting, but calm. The men continued to rub them as they dismounted. Grandfather looked at us, smiling, and said, "You can choose your horses now. Little Chief, I think your father has already chosen yours."

I knew this before Grandfather said it. Father sat astride a strong, black and white dappled stallion. The sleek, sweating horse was the most beautiful animal I'd ever seen. Already I caught myself talking in my mind to the horse. *We belong together,* I thought. *You were waiting for me, and I for you.*

I approached the horse and looked for the first time into his wide, brilliant eyes. The horse blinked and nickered and I, without thinking, nickered back. Then I reached a hand out to stroke his head. I sent my thoughts to the horse. *And what is a good name for you? A strong horse deserves a strong name, a good name.* I bent, pulled a handful of prairie grass from the earth, and fed my horse for the first time. I let him smell my head, my neck, my hands. The horse's name sounded in my mind the way the words of a song are caught. *Wasaka.* I heard it again. *Wasaka.* I put my arms around his neck and hugged him, thanking him for telling me his name.

Father smiled at me. "What do you think, Son?"

"*Wasaka.* His name is Wasaka."

He laughed, "Strong One. A good name for a strong horse. And you named him quickly."

I nodded. "I didn't name him. He told me his name."

"Ahh," my father hummed, "Also a good thing. Get on. I'll help."

I can hardly describe the feeling of climbing onto Wasaka for the first time. My father laced his fingers together to give me a place to put my foot, to gain the high back of my horse. It was as if I had ridden the strong back of my father all these years, and now he was giving me over to my horse. I sat astride Wasaka looking down at the face of my father—looking down—and yet I realized that no matter the course of my life, I would always be looking up to my father. It was the right way.

A clutch of emotion grabbed me across the chest and I resisted the urge to weep like a baby. Instead, I patted Wasaka's back, looked my father in the eye and said, "Thank you, Father."

10 Grandfather's Dream

When we returned to the village, Grandfather announced to all present that he once again wanted to talk to the whole village, that we would gather that night to celebrate the end of the horse camp—and the beginning of training for the new hunters. "And we will have a naming ceremony for one of your cousins."

The young man who was to get a name that night was Runs Fast, the one I had admired for so many years. He was a strong hunter, one with a special relationship with horses. I could still hear in my mind the way he'd said, "It is not hero's work, little cousin, to do what is necessary for the people."

I had heard many stories from Grandfather about Runs Fast. Even as a boy he was a strong hunter. From the time he first rode with the men he showed great skill and bravery, always racing ahead to kill the first buffalo. Grandfather also said this boy was very much like me—always in a hurry, a strong leader and that he had also left camp and gotten into plenty of trouble.

I was excited to see what name my cousin would be given. The men left that night and Runs Fast declared that he would shoot the buffalo for his own naming.

It was a long night. I yearned to be old enough to ride with the hunters, to climb on the back of Wasaka and hunt the buffalo.

The next day I again stacked wood into high mounds and helped the women prepare for yet a second feast. This time, there was no punishment, no ribbing—I just did the work necessary to help the people prepare. By early afternoon the fires were banked as the riders came into the camp, this time with three buffalo.

When the meal was nearly finished cooking, Grandfather Whirling Hand called us to the circle for the naming. The little children had picked up on the ongoing excitement and mothers had to calm them in order to begin the ceremony.

Grandfather held up an eagle feather that he said had come from his father's father. He called Runs Fast forward and sang songs and prayed over him. When the praying was done, he tied the feather in Runs Fast's hair and said, "I am giving this name to this boy because he shows no fear. He is a good hunter. Someday he will have his own band and be a great leader. *Wakan Tanka* showed me this name in the form of the white stallion guarding the wild herd. This horse will cross rivers, climb steep mountains to protect his herd. The stallion is willing to do anything to protect his herd—even if it is a crazy thing. So I would like to give this name to this boy. Crazy Horse. His name is now Crazy Horse." Grandfather began singing a song he made for this occasion.

When the naming was over, everyone's spirits were high. We ate, sang and danced until long after the sun had slid behind the hill and night had come.

Again I climbed the hillside behind the village to see the events from afar. I sat down on my boulder and watched. The moon shone brightly above the earth, full and round. Its light joined the light of the fire in the center of the dancing circle. It was a peaceful scene. The horse camp was over. I had my horse, and Runs Fast had gotten his name. But my thoughts, like a well-trained dog, returned to considering the plight of the white boy tied to a tree as punishment for what he could not help or change.

I wanted to climb on the back of Wasaka and go immediately to free Mato Ska. Impatience sizzled through me. If hunting and killing a buffalo was the next thing I must do before fulfilling the dream *Wakan Tanka* had given me, then I wanted to hunt the buffalo now, today. I wanted to go with Crazy Horse the next time the men hunted.

It was impossible to sit still any longer. I hurried back down the hill and found Grandfather. "Can I talk to you?"

"No. I know what you want to talk about—and I have given my answer. You have a horse now, but you must learn to ride that horse. And hunt. Think about your people, Little Chief, and not the White Bear. There are many of us. Soon we will have to split our village into several bands. People need much food, and the strong young men must provide that food. Put your mind on providing that food now, Little Chief."

I heard the scolding tone of Grandfather's voice and yet he smiled at me, a patient smile. It had been only days since Rabbit and I had returned. Grandfather was right. It was not yet time. "Yes, Grandfather," I said, feeling bad to have bothered him, but before I could leave, he stopped me.

"There is something else, Little Chief. I have also had dreams. It is time for me to tell those dreams to the people. Tomorrow night we will gather yet a third time so I can tell my dreams."

Others overheard and word circled the camp that there was to be yet a third night of feasting and stories. Grandfather was going to tell of his dreams.

I went to sleep full of anticipation that night. Dreams were powerful messages given to us to guide our steps, to show the way to the future, perhaps beyond. I knew this because *Wakan Tanka* had given me a dream and it had proven true. What would Grandfather's dreams foretell?

By dusk the next evening, I could scarcely bear the waiting. All day long I had thought about what Grandfather was going to tell us. My body went through fierce times of trembling and I now linked this shivering not with fever or sickness, but with dreams. This time we ate first, then Grandfather asked Rabbit to add wood to the fire. I helped him and soon the fire was crackling and sending small sparks out into the night to join their sisters, the stars. The people sat on robes around the blaze. The firelight cast an unearthly glow on their faces. The evening air pressed down from the heavens and the smoke lingered, hovering around us like spirits. I think I was not the only one who felt this humming, shivering thing.

When all were quiet, Grandfather picked up a drum and stick and began slowly with a song. He asked Crazy Horse and me to burn sage and smudge the people, to cleanse and bless this night. I walked the circle; the air was charged, but the burning sage seemed to chase the smoke from the fire away. When we finished, Grandfather pointed to a space beside him; Crazy Horse and I sat down.

He stood up. He pointed to me and began speaking. "When Little Chief and his cousin left the village they left because my grandson had had a dream. When they returned, he told me of a family of people who are not Lakota, who are different from other tribes we have met. These different people have pale skin. They cover their bodies with cloth. They build houses not like our own. And my grandson told me about a shining stick the man pointed into the air. Fire and thunder came from this stick. Grandson, show them the metal ball."

I dug in my pouch and pulled out the round metal ball he'd given to me. Grandfather took the ball and held it up for others to see, walking the circle so that all could see the unfamiliar object. He told them about his brother who had died from this small metal ball. When all had viewed it, he gave the ball back to me and sat down again.

He said, "This round metal is *maza*. This is something that is coming. In my dream, it comes as a big spider and I see the spider's web made of this metal. It will spread through all this land to the point where we, the Lakota people, have no place to go, nowhere to run." He took a long, slow breath. The people stared at him, their eyes gleaming in the firelight.

Grandfather's pain cut me in my chest. I felt his hurt. It shocked me. I had felt the pain of White Bear, and had often felt the pain of others, but never had I felt my Grandfather's pain like this. It frightened me.

He continued. "It begins. The spider is building his web. This webbing will trap the buffalo, the animals, and our people in its metal. It is coming and will hold us down." He looked slowly across the circle, raising his hand and pointing to the women who held babies close to their breasts. "Those babies in your arms, they will see it." He pointed to a row of strong, young hunters. "And they will not be able to stop it. Their yet unborn sons will try, they will fight to the death . . . and they will not stop it."

I watched the women. They no longer looked at Grandfather but had turned their eyes toward their little ones, pulling them closer as if to keep the spider's web from wrapping around their babies. I felt the pain and fear in them as well. Something tightened like a band of leather around the top of my head. My vision blurred. The light of the fire, the smoke, the cool night air seemed to recede and I felt alone . . . in a cave or a cloud. I had the confusing thought that I would be there to see these changes; that I would be on both sides of this webbing, this *maza* that spreads. I barely heard the rest of Grandfather's speech, so drawn inward was I.

I forced myself to listen again. Grandfather spoke about how the clans would divide again and again, each seeking safer grounds in small bands. Grandfather's pain pierced my heart with the next words, "Our great hunters, who kill now only for food and honor, will become not hunters but warriors. They will kill not only animals, but other human beings. This *maza*, this metal webbing, this biting spider will take this life we know away from us. Our hunters will be forced to hunt the ones who hold the thunder sticks. The thunder stick is more powerful than our bows."

My throat thickened. I saw tears gather in the eyes of the people, and I wanted to cry out against this thing that was coming.

Grandfather said, "Remember these words. *Wakan Tanka* did not put us here to kill. He put us here to share and get along; to share this land with the buffalo, with birds and other animals, with each other. *Wakan Tanka* looks down at us and he gives us Mother Earth, who carries us. A terrible time comes—I have seen it in my dream—a time when the *maza,* the webbing of the spider, will take much away from us. It will be difficult, but we can emerge on the other side. We will be *wasaka*—strong—if we remember we are kin with the earth, with animals, with each other. If we remember, we will emerge from the trouble strong once again."

With those words Grandfather again prayed and beat his drum. He sang a slow song, and his voice seemed to falter for a moment and then grow strong again. With its renewed strength, I felt the listeners grow strong again in spite of their great fear.

When Grandfather finished, I went to his side. Crazy Horse also stood and came to his other side. Together we helped him to his tipi. Grandfather's storytelling had taken his strength away.

11 The Buffalo Hunter

The rest of the summer I spent with the other boys who had been chosen to train with the older hunters. We worked our horses, practiced with our bows, and learned more about tracking. We gained strength and skill and prepared for the time when we would hunt the buffalo with the older hunters. Our training sessions were charged with energy, humming with purpose.

The younger children often gathered to watch us practice shooting. First we stuffed a deer hide with grass and straw and set it in the crook of a tree. We were working not just on a good aim, but how deeply we could drive the arrows. We also took turns shooting an arrow into the sky and following it with other arrows to see how close they would land together. Since the buffalo did not stand still and wait to be shot, we had to learn to shoot at moving things. Because of my previous months of practice, I was already a strong shooter. And the 'loose skin' Grandfather had teased me about made it easy for me to get inside of my horse and come to know him. Wasaka and I quickly became inseparable.

Sometimes when I stood on the river bank watering Wasaka, I would look up to see Grandfather watching me, his eyes filled with an intensity I could only guess at. He'd said no more about the spider's web, the *maza* that was coming. He had planted his dreams among us and then ceased to speak further about them.

I thought often of Grandfather's dream and what it meant. I didn't understand why I had dreamed of going to free the white bear—the boy whose father carried one of the thunder sticks. The *maza*, the spreading metal web, frightened me, so did the thunder stick, but these fears were not strong enough to root out the desire to free Mato Ska.

To sort my thoughts, I often climbed the hillside and gazed down into the village to think. I liked evenings best, when the smell of meat cooking and berry soup reached my nostrils, and the sounds of children playing and women talking reached my ears. I could not imagine the things Grandfather had spoken about—that the spider's web, this *maza*, could be powerful enough to interrupt such a peaceful life as the one I saw below. He said our people had lived this way for thousands of years, sometimes traveling, sometimes staying in one place.

A sense of urgency grew in my heart. While I practiced, or rode, or slept I thought of what I must do. I prayed often to *Wakan Tanka* to tell me the right time to travel again to the shelter made of logs, to the tree where the punished boy was sitting. In my mind, the boy was tied there day and night; probably it was not so, but this image was fixed in my mind.

The winter passed slowly, so slowly, and then it was spring and then summer again and our training continued. I was now twelve; old enough, I thought, to hunt the buffalo. I remained patient as long as I could, but when the earth baked dry beneath the burning sun of late summer and the grasses turned yellow once again, my impatience grew. The hunters ranged farther and farther to find the green shoots and grasses their horses liked best, and to hunt for the people. I knew we would soon break camp and move, following the buffalo to new grounds. I could not imagine going another full winter without doing what I needed to do. I had a strong horse now; I had a stronger bow; I was a good shot. It was time.

At last I approached Grandfather's tipi after the evening meal and stories had ended, when the dry night air began to cool. I smelled the season beginning to change and could not wait any longer.

He sat on a robe outside the door of his tipi when I approached him. "Grandfather, I would like to speak with you."

He stood up and said, "Good. Let's walk up the hill, Grandson, to the place where you spend your evenings." He smiled, letting me know he had been watching my movements the past few months.

Although he was the Elder of the village, there was no infirmity in his body. His strong legs and sure feet easily climbed the hill to the boulder I liked to sit on. The sky still held light but a full moon rose over the horizon. It was beautiful. The chill air had encouraged the people to light small fires for the night. Down below, the fires in each tipi glowed like small moons. I saw people in circles talking around dying fires, the older children still playing hunter with sticks and thin sinew, the women nursing their babies one more time before bed.

"Grandfather," I said at last. "I am restless. When can I learn to kill a buffalo? I cannot rest because I keep thinking about the white boy. It hurts my chest, Grandfather. It hurts my heart thinking about him. I need to free the white bear of my dreams and I've been thinking about what to do once I free him." I looked at him, watching his reaction. "I want to bring that white boy here, to our village. I want to teach him, show him how we live. He doesn't have a good life there. He is treated badly. Our people would not treat him that way. I want to teach him to hunt, to help him grow strong so he can go back and show his people that he is a good man."

Grandfather laughed softly. "That is another reason you have been called Little Chief. You ask good questions. You think about things. You are curious."

The next words did not come easily to my tongue. "I need to go alone, Grandfather. I can't take anybody else with me. I can't endanger Rabbit or any of our hunters with that *maza*, that thunder stick. I want to go alone, and I want to go soon."

"I see." Quiet now, he looked out across the village and beyond, thinking it seemed, and staring straight into the spirit realm. "I have watched you, Grandson. It is time now for you young hunters to learn to kill the buffalo. You must show me that you are a good hunter, and then I will agree. Tomorrow we will hunt."

That night, I could barely close my eyes. Tomorrow I would hunt the buffalo. If I was successful, if I was a good hunter, I would ride south in search of Mato Ska once again. I prayed to *Wakan Tanka* to make the hunt a good one. *Hear me, Wakan Tanka. Help Wasaka and me work together, to hunt well so that I can go and do this thing which you have shown me in a dream. Help us, Wakan Tanka.*

From the moment my eyes opened the next morning, I knew I would be successful. I felt it in my belly. The call went out almost before the sun rose, and by early morning we had gathered our weapons and mounted our horses. Rabbit was there. I was glad we would make our first hunt together. The women brought packs of food and supplies for us to take along, as the ride would be long and hard.

Before we rode out, I watched Grandfather go over to the older boy who always sat near his tipi drawing with a stick in the dirt. He talked to the boy for a long while, watching closely as he drew lines, raising his hand to point toward the north and west, and drawing again. Grandfather nodded, and then touched the boy's shoulder. He looked pleased and walked to his horse, mounted, and said, "Now we ride."

There were twenty of us. Crazy Horse and four of his friends rode ahead. It was as if he was already leading his own band of hunters. Grandfather, the older hunters, and we four younger men who had been included in the hunt rode behind at a slower pace. My father was there. And Rabbit's father. I felt proud to be riding out of the village with the men, the women calling their goodbyes behind us. Wasaka felt strong beneath my thighs. I stroked his neck and talked to him in my mind about killing our first buffalo. He whinnied, as if hearing my thoughts. I rode up beside Grandfather and asked him, "What did that boy tell you?"

His eyes lit up and he smiled. He said, "That one, although he never leaves the village to ride and hunt, is a great hunter. He sits and listens to all the stories. He has mapped the movement of the buffalo herds, the lay of the land, for many seasons. He knows exactly where we can find our herd."

I was stunned. This boy who ate, who sat, who did not ride or play, was a great hunter? I could scarcely absorb what Grandfather had said. I thought again of the white boy and wondered what gifts, what wonders, were hiding in his slow gait, his weaknesses.

After that I rode in silence, keeping my distance from the high spirits of the other younger hunters. I focused all thought on the hunt.

Today I would kill a buffalo. I felt it in my bones. Today I would gain Grandfather's permission to leave, to pursue the task ahead of me.

After a long morning's ride, we reached a steep hillside, which ended at a high ridge. There we dismounted, rested the horses, and a plan was made. My father dispatched a quick rider to the top of the hill to see if the sitting boy's prediction was correct. I hadn't realized my father was leading this hunt. I went to Grandfather and said, "I thought you would be in charge."

He pointed at my father's retreating back. "Why would I be in charge when I have a Charging Bull?" He laughed at his own joke and said, "I am old, Little Chief.   I have not hunted in many, many years. I am along only to watch over small boys, to make sure they don't get themselves killed."

Grandfather's words poked at me a bit. He had come to babysit us. But then I thought of how carefully he'd worked over the past many weeks, to teach us to be strong hunters, and I forgave him the jab.

Before long, the rider raced down the slope smiling and waving wildly, but saying nothing. His silence told us the herd was just beyond the ridge, in the valley below. The scout dismounted and said it was a big herd—more than he could count. The plan called for the most experienced hunters to circle the ridge, placing themselves on the far side of the valley and chasing the herd south. Crazy Horse and his band would hunt and kill what they could from the main herd and then cut a smaller herd off for us younger, inexperienced hunters to hunt.

Tension hummed through our group. The older riders left and Grandfather gathered us around him. We'd heard these instructions many times but he spoke them again. "Ride up behind the buffalo, keeping close but not going directly toward him. When you are neck-to-neck, get close and drive your arrow deep into his front quarter. Then get out of the way as fast as you can. This animal is dangerous and unpredictable." When he finished the instructions, he lay down on the ground as if taking a nap.

I thought this strange and said, "Grandfather, if you fall asleep, you may not be able to get on your horse fast enough."

He patted the earth. "I am listening, Grandson. Get down. The earth speaks to those willing to listen."

Rabbit and I and the other young hunters got down and put our ears to the earth. A nearby horse stomped the ground. We were amazed at how clear the sound traveled. While we lay listening, Grandfather told us to remember that the horse is as much the hunter as the man. "You must work with your horse in order to kill the buffalo. You must trust each other. Show no fear, ride from behind, trust your horse, and drive your arrow deep."

I looked at my childhood friends, at Grandfather lying on the ground, at the birds flying high above and I thought we must look like a bunch of lazy, crazy men napping beneath a burning sun on the low side of a hill. Then I felt the rumble. With my ear to the ground, I heard and felt the buffalo coming. My heart sped up, my hands were suddenly sweaty with excitement. Soon. It would be soon.

Grandfather got up, waved us onto our horses and pointed, without talking, to the top of the ridge. He turned and rode up the hill.

I stroked Wasaka's mane and neck. I reached farther down along his side feeling the strength of his body and whispered, "You are part of me. I am part of you. We will go together and do this thing." Wasaka raised his head as if listening—no, as if hearing. He huffed and snorted, tossing his head in a way that made me laugh.

Topping the ridge, we saw below two gigantic herds. One moved from the north, chased by the older riders, and one ate and rested on the valley floor. I had never, ever seen so many buffalo. It was a sight I will never forget. How I wish I could have frozen time in that moment, to hold that feeling, that sight—but time did not agree. Crazy Horse and his band rode hard and fast to the west and the hunt was on. Grandfather pointed and said, "Look. There is the bull."

On the outer edge of the herd was a huge bull buffalo. It was clearly the leader of the moving herd. The bull was a giant, several hands taller than the other animals. Crazy Horse rode closer to the herd. Unbelievably, he'd chosen that bull buffalo as his prey.

Three hunters each brought down a buffalo. The herd became frenzied, frightened at the smell of the blood of their own. Four more riders came up fast alongside a buffalo—three of them made their kill.

Crazy Horse, riding a white and gray stallion, came up behind that bull buffalo. When he was nearly neck-to-neck, he pulled his bow and sunk an arrow into the animal's front quarter. The bull buffalo roared and pulled to the side. We watched, horrified, as Crazy Horse did not pull out of the way fast enough and the bull buffalo charged, ramming his head into his horse. Time again twisted and seemed to slow as we watched. Both horse and man went down. My breath caught in my chest. The bull stopped, turned, and eyed the downed horse and rider. Crazy Horse got up. A rider from his band rode up behind him, ready to help. The bull huffed and snorted, ready to charge. Crazy Horse spoke to his mount and the horse got up. He jumped on its back, grabbed the other rider's spear, and met the bull's charge with one of his own.

A wild shriek split the air as Crazy Horse drove the spear into the buffalo's back. We were unsure if it was man or beast that shrieked. We were watching two great warriors in battle. The bull buffalo was strong. He was angry. Crazy Horse pulled clear and the animal went down, but not all the way down. The bull buffalo sat on one hindquarter, snorting. It was angry, but weakening. It tried to stand but collapsed again. Crazy Horse made a small circle and then turned again to face his opponent.

Grandfather said, "It's not over yet. Watch. He is going for his knife."

The animal gained its feet once again and Crazy Horse's mount turned toward the bull and charged it with its head. When horse and buffalo collided, Crazy Horse jumped onto the back of the giant bull and drove his knife again and again into the animal's neck until it collapsed, and died.

Crazy Horse disappeared on the other side of the animal and when he reappeared, he held the beast's bloody heart. He gave a spine-tingling yell, took a bite, and held the heart toward the heavens. A wild cry went out among the other hunters and each resumed the hunt, taking down one, and another, and another of the herd. Several of the hunters did as Crazy Horse had done, slitting the side of the buffalo, cutting out the heart, taking a bite, then raising the bloody heart in offering to *Wakan Tanka*. The cries of horse and hunter, the falling buffalo, the speed of the hunters, their arrows flying, it was like nothing I had ever seen or felt.

Finally, Crazy Horse's band of hunters cut thirty or more buffalo from the herd and drove them south away from the main herd. Grandfather said, "Prepare. Remember all I have told you, and work with your horses. Go now and be safe."

It was almost a relief to kick the side of my horse and ride like lightning down the side of that hill and into that valley. I was fired up. Wasaka was fired up. I chose a midsized female, nothing like the giant bull Crazy Horse had brought down. I focused my energy, doing exactly as I had learned. I sped up my horse until Wasaka and I were nearly neck and neck with the female. I drew my bow, pulled hard, hard, harder on it, and then drove my arrow deep into the front quarter of the buffalo, just behind its shoulder. I pulled right as fast as I could.

The buffalo went down in a tumble of dust and snorting. The rest of the herd ran on. My heart thundered in my chest and I heard the cry of the other hunters, felt the sweat trickle down my back. It was a clean kill.

I dismounted and pulled my knife through the buffalo's neck to bleed her out. I did not slit the side or take the heart. That was for another time. Wasaka danced nervously nearby, and I ran to him, praising him for his good work, his quickness. The horse whinnied and snorted. I rubbed his neck furiously, as much to calm myself as to calm Wasaka.

The rest of the day and the next passed in a blur. We younger hunters were given the task of gutting the buffalo, stripping the hides, and cutting up the meat. The hunters watched us, instructing our blades, teasing us when we were covered head to toe with blood, our hands sticky and wet. They said the coyotes would probably carry us off that night, mistaking us for carrion. It was a terrible job, but we did it without complaint. We had to pull the entrails from the bellies; take the bladders and wash them quickly so they would not spoil; take the hearts, the livers, the brains, the tongues and place them each separately into sacks. Even the intestines had to be cleaned quickly to make them good for later use. Once I looked up and Rabbit really did look like some dead thing the birds had abandoned. I must have looked the same. When we finally slid into the creek to wash off, I couldn't scrub hard enough. The smell of blood and gore stuck in my nose for days after.

The older hunters took choice parts from the buffalo and cooked them over the evening fire to celebrate. There was much work to be done. We had killed twenty buffalo, a good hunt. All the meat and hides had to be prepared to take back to the village where the women would then take over the preparations.

All but three of us younger hunters had killed their first buffalo. Rabbit was one who did not get his first kill. Crazy Horse's encounter with the bull buffalo had so terrified him that our Grandfather would not let him hunt. Rabbit was ashamed but Grandfather told him these things were in the hands of *Wakan Tanka*—we could not force our way into manhood.

While we prepared the buffalo, Rabbit was quiet, working beside me. I wanted to say something to him, to comfort him, but no words came. The older hunters had been silent—not teasing or making jokes about Rabbit's fear. I thought again how our people did not attack weakness—only strength.

The night before we were to return to the village, I found Rabbit beside a swampy pool of water. He was staring into the green water, tossing small sticks and rocks to ripple the placid surface. I tried to make a joke. "Not thinking of drinking that stuff are you?"

He said nothing.

"Come on, *tanhansi*. There is no shame in waiting a bit longer to hunt your first buffalo."

"You didn't hesitate. You were not afraid."

What could I say to that? There was nothing.

Rabbit said, "Now you will go alone to free the white bear. Grandfather said you could go when you had killed a buffalo."

"I was going to go alone anyway. I told Grandfather this and he agreed. I should not have taken you along the first time. It is better this way."

He turned and faced me. "Why? Because you would not want a 'girl' riding with you?"

A spur of anger jabbed me. "I don't think of you as a girl. I never have. It is you who calls yourself this." Our friendship had changed suddenly and become strained and distant. If it hadn't changed, I would have wrestled him to the ground and pummeled his head for being such a baby, for feeling sorry for himself. Now, I just stood and watched him, saying nothing more.

"Leave me alone, Little Chief. Go rescue your white bear. Go alone then."

I walked away, leaving him beside the green pond, feeling as if I had left childhood behind; the games, the wrestling, the pranks—the friendship. Rabbit was a part of that time of my life, and now it was changing. I couldn't turn back, and was uncertain about how to go forward. I left him standing there.

And I couldn't get the picture out of my mind of Crazy Horse charging that bull.

12 This Time I Go Alone

Early the next day we loaded the meat and hides onto our horses and rode back to the main camp. The people greeted us as we crossed the river and there was much cheering and laughing. Grandfather told them all to prepare for a great feast with singing and dancing that night.

My mother met us at the river. She hugged me, clearly relieved that both her husband and son were unharmed—and that I had killed my first buffalo.

She stood back and said, "I think I am losing a son."

"No, Mother. I am back." I grinned and pointed to my body. "I didn't lose anything."

She took me by the shoulders and said, "I can see that. I meant I have lost a son—but our village has gained another hunter. I am proud of you, Little Chief."

My tongue would not work. I could not say a word and just stood before my mother until she gave a small laugh, and turned and went back to her work.

Spirits were high that night. The village had plenty of meat, and all of its hunters had returned unharmed. When we had eaten our fill, Grandfather gathered us together and said he wanted to speak.

I did not sit with the children that night. I sat with the hunters. It seemed significant; my place in the village had changed when the buffalo fell beneath my arrow.

Grandfather stood and spoke, "I want to tell you what I witnessed during the hunt. Listen carefully. We honor two of our hunters tonight. Each of them performed well and has earned a feather."

I admit that when he said those words, I harbored the childish wish that I would be one of the hunters given a feather this night. Now I realize I had done nothing extraordinary, nothing to win such a prize. No, Grandfather told the village of Crazy Horse's fearless encounter with the giant bull buffalo, and then invited him to speak.

Crazy Horse told the people he did not perform this without his horse—and his weapons. "And there is one other person who helped me defeat the bull buffalo," he said to us. "When I was down, he came to me and gave me his spear. He didn't get a buffalo—because he protected me. I want to give the hide of the bull buffalo to Standing Bear and his family—and the meat to any family who has not enough meat."

Standing Bear stood up and went to Crazy Horse. "Thank you, *Kola.*"

"No, thank you."

The two men stared at each other for a long moment. Crazy Horse had performed a great feat, and yet he did not boast or swagger, he did not act prideful. Again, in my heart, I prayed to *Wakan Tanka* to make me such a hunter.

Standing Bear turned to us and said, "I witnessed the actions of a great hunter today. I will tell his story to my children and they will tell it to their children. We will never forget what we have seen."

Grandfather honored Crazy Horse with an eagle feather and then, much to our surprise, he took the other feather and crossed to the young man who was known to spend all of his days sitting in front of his tipi. He was a large boy, nearly a man, and yet he did not ride or hunt.

He said, "Stand, my grandson."

The young man stood. He looked shy, and a bit confused.

Grandfather said, "His family has asked me to give him a Lakota name and *Wakan Tanka* gave me this name during the hunt yesterday when I saw the bull buffalo so angry and proud, sitting on the earth still trying to protect his herd. Just as the stallion gave me the name for Crazy Horse, so this bull buffalo gave me a name for this boy who sits. It is because he sits and listens that he knows all the land, the movements of the herds, the way the birds fly overhead— all of these things he keeps in his head to be used later. It is because of this boy that we have meat tonight. I give him the name Sitting Bull. This young hunter will one day be a great leader who uses his mind." He fixed the feather in the boy's hair. "I give this eagle feather to you who sits and listens, to Sitting Bull."

The people were stunned. They erupted into cheers and cries, and Sitting Bull had a silly grin on his face. He reached up and stroked the smooth feather now dangling from his braid. We had all known this boy was different, but it was simply accepted. To have him so honored by our Elder was a surprise. Crazy Horse and the other hunters went and clapped his back or shook his hand while Sitting Bull's parents stood to one side and looked on proudly.

With a sharp rap on the drum and the call of men's voices singing out into the evening, the dancing began. I knew it would go on for many hours, so high were the spirits of the people. They would dance until the little ones curled onto buffalo robes near the fire and fell asleep.

I walked to the edge of the camp where I could see the festivities, and yet was apart from them. For the other young hunters, killing their first buffalo was an end point, a height to be gained. For me, it was only a beginning. It signaled the freedom I needed to leave the village and travel alone to do what my dream demanded I do. I felt strong, and proud, and ready. I also felt anxious to be off. As I stood there, the night sky seemed to press down on me. This need to act on the dream given by *Wakan Tanka* was like a weight on my shoulders. A figure emerged from the shadows. It was Crazy Horse.

"I watched you bring down your buffalo, Little Chief."

"You did?" Somehow the idea that a great hunter like Crazy Horse would notice a boy like me was startling.

He laughed. "Yes, it was a good kill. You performed well." He sat down and patted the earth next to him. I sat down beside him. "Something troubles you, Little Chief, something that takes you from the warm fire of your people. What is it?"

I didn't know what to say, so I told him the truth, that the dream of the white bear was like a spirit haunting me— that it was all I thought about. Crazy Horse listened without asking any questions, without comment. I told him, "Grandfather said I could go to do this thing when I had a stronger horse, when I had killed my first buffalo. I want to go now."

I saw him nod, his head outlined in the distant glow of the fire. He looked at me then and said, "We all have our path to walk, Little Chief. I had thought to bring you into my circle, to have you ride with us, but I hear now there is another trail you must follow. Go. Talk to your Grandfather. And if there is anything I can do to help, let me know."

He left then, just as silently as he had come, and I was alone in the dark with only my thoughts. Crazy Horse's attention touched my heart. Tears gathered in my eyes. I had wondered if this dream that dogged my tracks was a foolish thing, a thing of childhood. Somehow having Crazy Horse take it seriously made me take it more seriously. If the dream was not from *Wakan Tanka,* it would leave me, this powerful need to free Mato Ska.

I circled the camp and walked to where Grandfather sat near the fire watching the dancers. I sat on the ground beside him and said, "Grandfather, I would like to speak to you."

"Why does that not surprise me, *Takoja.*" His smile looked almost sad. "Come to my tipi later and we will talk."

"Yes, Grandfather. I will come."

The familiar shiver began racing up my arms and legs again. Soon, maybe even the next day, I would leave my mother's tipi and travel alone to do what I had been set to do. So long had I thought about it, now that the time was near, I could hardly believe it. I looked up at the heavens. Thin clouds moved across the dim curtain of sky. Soon I would be traveling, just like those clouds.

Where would this dream take me? What would happen? How would I free that white bear? So many questions; I could answer none of them. The words of the song that had come the first time I traveled to see the white family returned to my mind now. I sang it aloud, softly. It soothed me, easing the shivering out of my body.

I have no ears, *Tunkasila*
Until you speak, *Tunkasila.*
I have no eyes, no eyes to see,
Until you look, *Tunkasila.*
My voice has no words but your words,
Hear my words, *Tunkasila.*
Hear my plea.

As I sang, a second voice joined mine. I turned and saw Rabbit emerge from the shadow near the ring of tipis.

He said, "I heard your song."

"It is my song now, isn't it."

Rabbit smiled. "You killed a buffalo, Little Chief."

"I know. It was a good thing."

My cousin stared at me a moment and then said, "I acted like such a boy. It was not time for me to kill my buffalo yet. That is all. It was your time. But instead of celebrating with you, I acted like a crying baby."

I didn't say anything; I just let the night absorb his admission.

"You're going soon, aren't you?" Rabbit said. "I want to come with you again, Little Chief."

"No, Cousin. This time I go alone. I must."

I expected Rabbit to argue, but he just nodded and said. "I thought so. I'll be here when you get back."

Like Crazy Horse, Rabbit too disappeared back into the shadows before I could say anything further. We are both growing up, I thought. We are becoming men now. It seemed as if many seasons had passed since Rabbit and I had foolishly crept out of the village to go south to find the different kind of people. In fact, only a few moons had passed. Then it was a child's game. Now, it felt larger somehow. I knew there would be dangers, and yet I was driven to undertake it. Life was sometimes mysterious.

I hesitated at the opening to Grandfather's tipi somehow knowing that once I slipped through that flap and gained his permission, my life would change in ways I could not yet even fathom. No longer would I be a boy, but a man entering some new, unknown world. With a deep, shaking breath I called out to him.

Grandfather told me to come in. When I dipped my head and entered, I saw the pipe beside him and knew he had been praying. He said when he put the *k'nik k'nik*, the sacred tobacco, in his pipe he was gathering the power from the six directions and placing them into the belly of Grandmother Earth. Smoking, Grandfather had told me, focused and strengthened his prayers.

"Can I talk with you, Grandfather?" I asked him quietly, not wanting to disturb his prayers.

"Sit down, T*akoja*. I know what it is you want to talk about. You have had a dream. You want to do as the dream has directed you—to free the white bear."

All hesitation fled as I settled beside him. Once again I told Grandfather of my dream, and about the powerful urge I had to free that white boy tied by the creek. "I need to do it, Grandfather. I know I'm still young, but I have killed a buffalo now and I must go. Somehow Mato Ska is connected to us, the Lakota people. I don't understand how but I keep thinking of the words you said about the *maza*, about the spider's web trapping our people. I don't want Crazy Horse and Sitting Bull to become warriors instead of hunters, to kill humans instead of animals. I want to stop that from happening."

He shook his head at me. "My grandson, there are many things you do not yet understand. You are in many ways still a boy, although you have performed well. But this . . . what is coming . . . you cannot stop. If you lived and died, and lived and died five times over, you would not yet gain the strength to stop it. I have seen it. I have told the people this."

"Then why, Grandfather? Why has *Wakan Tanka* given me this dream? Why has he sent me to rescue this white boy whose father carries a thunder stick?" I felt all the anxiety, all the fear and power that had driven me for so long, gather in my throat and I felt like wailing like a baby. My throat was thick and my stomach tight, as if I'd sent my question straight to *Wakan Tanka*.

"We don't always know these things, Grandson. We can't always see out far enough to understand the bigger sweep of time . . . of events. We can only pray and act in this time. And you are right. It is time for you to do what *Wakan Tanka* has told you to do. Go and tell your mother and father I have said it's time for you to go. Tell them I have agreed to your journey."

With those words, he seemed to droop into his buffalo robe, as if the mass and strength of his body had gone up the tipi hole with the smoke from his fire. This was also hard, I thought, to leave my Grandfather, to leave my parents' tipi, to go alone. I took a long breath, crushing the fear down before it could crush me, and I said, "Grandfather, I don't want anyone to follow me. *Wakan Tanka* will be with me. I keep him in my heart. Just pray for me, but don't send anyone to help or protect me. I do this alone. I'll go now and let you rest. I'll tell Mother and Father, and then I will leave early in the morning."

Grandfather took my hands and held them, looking deeply into my eyes. I knew he wanted to shelter me, to send strong hunters along to protect me.

I said, "Trust me, Grandfather. I will ride alone. I'll be back with the boy. And if I have not returned by the sixth day, then you can send riders to look for me."

He dropped my hands and nodded. "Good night then, Grandson. Be safe."

"I will, Grandfather."

I hurried through the nearly empty camp and went to our tipi. My parents were sitting outside beneath the bright moonlight as if waiting for me. I told them my plans and that Grandfather had agreed. I told them I was nearly grown and would soon need my own tipi. There were no protests, no arguments. Mother went silently to pack food for my trip. Left alone with my father, I felt as if my heart sought something from this man who had sheltered and protected me through so many seasons. "Father?"

"No, Son. You don't need my permission to do what your heart directs you to do. I have watched you. I see this is what you must do." And then, as if the words cost him some effort, he said, "I am proud of you, Little Chief. Go—and be safe."

For the second time that evening, my throat thickened, making further words impossible. I nodded and slipped into the tipi to sleep. I lay on my back for a long time staring out the tipi hole at the stars above. My parents whispered together outside the flap. I heard my mother cry, my father's gentle words comforting her. Tears collected in my own eyes and wet the sides of my face. I wondered if it was the fate of all sons to one day make their mothers cry.

I slept in fits and starts that night, sometimes coming full awake and remembering that this was the day I had waited for. My body hummed with excitement but I told myself rest was the first need of a great hunter. I forced my body to sleep.

13 The Second Journey South

The sky was not yet tinged with even the faintest glow of morning light when I rose. I rolled my buffalo robe into a bundle, picked up my pack, bow, and arrows, and walked quietly to my horse. Part of me wanted to crawl back into the tipi, to bury myself beneath the soft layers of my childhood. But I mounted, gave Wasaka a nudge, and rode out of the village.

I headed south. When I topped the rise, the watchman met me and we shook hands. He asked if I wanted company on this day's ride and I said, "No, I go alone today."

There are no words to describe how I felt that early morning with the safety and protection of my village and my people falling behind me. My throat prickled, as if I'd swallowed a cactus. Everything in me wanted to turn and flee toward home once again, toward my parents' safe surround. Then, the longer I rode, the more my senses awakened. I began noticing things, small things. I noticed the abundance of grass, the quick darting of rabbit, bird, fox. I heard the wind call to the birds—the birds call back. I smelled sagebrush baking in the rising heat of the sun, the perfume of Grandmother Earth. It struck my nostrils and I sucked through my mouth, tasting the sage. Wasaka snorted and I laughed aloud. His nose, it seemed, was connected to mine.   My fear evaporated and I was no longer small but a part of all I saw around me, sheltered and protected by *Wakan Tanka*, by my dream. I took my flute out of my pack and played to the wind, to the birds, to the loneliness. It soothed me.

Once I disturbed a rattlesnake sunning itself on a rocky outcropping. I had dismounted and was squatting down to relieve the tension in my backside when I saw it nearly at my feet. Its stony eyes met mine, and we stared at each other for a long time, as if each deciding whether the other was friend or foe or food. I considered taking him for my supper but somehow joined my own loneliness with his; my skin became a snakeskin for just a brief flash of time. He slithered off—and I slithered off.

I rode through the day and late into the night before I camped. Now I can admit it was not haste, but fear, that kept me riding. I had never spent a night alone before. When I finally made camp, it was a lonely thing. Every sound in the night magnified again and again. The sky looked inky, the trees foreign and frightening. A strong wind blew and its howl made me wonder about spirits riding the treetops. Fortunately my lack of sleep the night before, combined with my sheer exhaustion, brought sleep quickly once I tumbled onto my buffalo robe.

The next day, alone with my thoughts and the wide land, I slid into a silence as big as the sky. The turmoil and tumble of my thoughts quieted. I simply moved south, always south, toward my fate.

The day was cool, the sky threaded with dense clouds, and it made for easy riding. Wasaka moved across the land with ease and speed and, by late afternoon of the second day, I reached the steaming river.

The cut of the land looked familiar, so often had I seen it in my dreams and thoughts. I eased off Wasaka and, staying under cover, walked the final distance. When I reached the place beside the creek where the boy had been tied, it was empty. I waited and waited but saw nothing. To gain a better vantage point, I crossed the creek and quietly made my way north into a stand of pine trees on a low ridge where I had a view of both the creek bank and the cabin. Maybe they no longer tied the boy, maybe he'd been somehow freed already, I thought. This had never occurred to me, that other events could have intervened in my absence. The homestead was oddly silent.

There was nothing to do but wait, and watch, and see what happened. I scouted the area and found a small indent in the ridge. It was not a cave exactly, more a hole in the cliff that rose above the hillside, but I decided it would make a good shelter.

Keeping an eye on the cabin and working quietly, I found some felled branches and used them to cover the part of the cave that was open to the sky. The day was waning and darkness coming quickly. I ate some food and then brought my buffalo robe and spread it on the floor of the small shelter. To the south, the prairie spread out and I watched the night unfold over the land. After riding so hard the past two days, I was bone tired. Within minutes of stretching out on the buffalo robe, I slept.

A terrible shrieking sound nearly lifted me off the ground the next morning. I awoke trembling and reaching for my bow. The sky was pale and I listened, ears cocked for signs of danger—or for the source of the terrible sound. Taking great care, I emerged from the alcove and scanned the area. Nothing.

I went to Wasaka and ran my hands across the horse's body, up and down his legs to make sure he was all right. Relieved to find no sign of snakebite or injury, I looked toward the homestead. To the west of the cabin there were several other buildings and one was an enclosure full of large birds. As I watched, a male bird, red and brown with a silly looking peak on its head, hopped up on a box and made that terrible sound.

Laughing, I felt foolish and whispered to my horse. "A bird, Wasaka. It is only a foolish bird ripping me out of a sound sleep." Smoke now curled up from the top of the cabin and I knew the people must be waking up.

I sat on a stony perch not unlike the boulder from which I viewed my village, only now I was days from home and alone. As I watched, the man came out of the cabin and went to work on a stack of logs. He had a long knife or blade and was pulling the bark off each log to reveal the pale wood beneath. The two brothers came out carrying a basket. They walked toward the birds, pulled open a part of the metal web enclosing them, and went in.

The metal web made me nervous. I thought of the spider, and the *maza* Grandfather had talked about, and shivered in the morning chill. The boys, however, began plucking something out of the corners of the bird house; they were collecting the eggs from the large birds. Again I grinned at my own fears. I childishly continued to see meaning in the simplest of things, a caw of a bird, the wire mesh, two boys gathering eggs.

This was a family not unlike my family, following their normal morning routine. The boys carried the basket inside and returned with a large white bowl. They poured water from a bucket and bathed themselves. The father came and also washed, and then all went back inside. I assumed they were having a meal and my stomach rumbled, reminding me I had not yet eaten.

I went back to my camp, had a bite of meat, and waited. Soon the boys and their father re-emerged and went to work on the log pile. It seemed they were building a second structure and I wondered why. Maybe one of the boys was going to take a wife. I looked around and wondered where they would find a wife in all this emptiness. The thought amused me. I also realized the two boys were my age—a little young to take a wife.

At last the mother came out of the cabin and offered the men a drink from a bucket. She was plain, pale, covered to her toes in a long skirt and a cap on her head shielding her eyes from the sun's glare. Beneath the cap her hair was as yellow as sunlight. I'd never seen such pale, golden hair, and it fascinated me. The boys had hair of a similar color, but the father's was darker, not the color of night sky like my people, but more the color of pine bark. The hair on his face was the same color. Occasionally the man straightened and stretched, grabbing the hair on his chin in a fist and tugging on it.

As if memorizing each detail for later use, I watched, wanting to know everything about this different kind of people so I could tell Grandfather what I had learned. When Rabbit and I had come the first time, everything had moved so fast there had not been time to observe and memorize anything.

While I watched, the scene below suddenly shifted. The slow brother, my Mato Ska, held himself down low and said something to his father. The father pointed to a little shelter and hollered. The boy ran over to the little house— I figured it must be a place to relieve himself, but when the boy reached the little house, he sneaked behind the little house, and came back out without having entered.

Something was not right. I noticed the boy's clothes were wet—he had wet himself—but that didn't make sense. He could have made it into the little house, or opened his pants and wet the grass. Instead, he had wet his own clothes. This was what had caused his father to tie him to the tree before.

My interest sharpened. I watched to see what would happen, wondering why the boy had done this intentionally. He left the little house and walked slowly toward his father. The stronger brother saw him, saw what he had done, and with a glance at his father, he went to the awkward brother and was talking, pointing toward the house as if urging him to go inside before the father saw.

No good. The father turned, dropped his hammer, and suddenly the peaceful scene shattered. The father started yelling and hollering. The mother came running out of the house just as the man grabbed the boy, landed a hand on his backside, and began dragging him toward the creek. I hunkered down deeper into the undergrowth. I was well sheltered, but the man's anger made me cautious, although I saw no sign of the thunder stick. When they reached the creek, the man hollered again. The other brother came running down. The father pointed toward the rope and he forced the stronger brother to tie his slower brother to the tree on the creek bank.

I understood none of what was being said. The words were another language, but I knew the language of human emotion—and the father's anger ruled this family. The mother and brother were at its mercy. The boy I had already named Mato Ska had no power at all. Soon the father herded the mother and other brother back up the slope to the cabin, leaving White Bear alone and tied.

I saw his scabbed neck, just as I'd seen the blood on the bear's neck in my dream. Mato Ska was peaceful now, listening to the birds, watching the water flow down stream, and drawing circles in the dirt with his finger. That was when I understood—the boy had wet himself purposely in order to be removed from his father's anger, to be free to sit beside the creek.

How can I approach him without scaring him, I wondered? The last time I revealed myself, the boy had screamed. That time I'd smeared my face with mud and stupidly let him see me. I must have looked like an animal spirit. I'd be more careful this time. I slipped quietly back to my shelter and got my flute. The boy seemed to like listening to water flowing and birds singing; maybe I could use my flute, become part of the natural sounds he already found soothing. I remembered the calm way the hunters had tamed the wild horses.

I stayed up near the cave watching until I saw the others go back inside the cabin. They would once again be occupied with eating a meal. It was clear White Bear was not to be included in this meal. I padded quietly down the slope and approached the creek from the bank opposite from where he was tied. I stayed hidden, but lifted my flute to my mouth and began playing. The tones were so low and unchanging they might have been wind in the trees. The boy's head came up. He listened. I sent a quick prayer to *Wakan Tanka* and continued playing, softly at first, moving the tones up and down as slow as the water moving in the steaming river. My heart pumped; the music of my flute quivered with my uneven breathing.

White Bear looked around as if trying to identify the source of the music. He listened. His face relaxed and he smiled as if the sound pleased him. This gave me courage, and relief. Perhaps I'd found the right way to approach him. I played the flute for a long time, remaining hidden in the undergrowth where he could not see me. Finally, with a last glance toward the cabin to make sure we were still alone, I stepped out of the undergrowth and approached the creek. I played and played, sending the calming music out to Mato Ska. His eyes widened as he saw me at last. I stepped to the edge of the water, still playing the flute.

He did not seem afraid this time. He listened, looking first at the flute and then at my face. Cautiously, I crossed the creek and came within three feet of him. I lowered the flute from my lips only long enough to smile at Mato Ska, to let him know I intended no harm. He reached a hand out and touched the tip of my moccasin as if petting an animal, and then he reached up and touched the end of the wooden flute and smiled back.

I sat down beside him and showed him the palm of my hand—flat, no knife or weapon. White Bear opened his palm and laid it atop mine. Encouraged, I reached out and touched his scabbed neck; shaking my head slightly to let him know I understood the hurt that rope had caused him.

I was as strange and unfamiliar to this boy as he was to me. He touched the leather of my shirt. I touched the soft cloth of his shirt. Our exploration of each other was like two animals sniffing each other's scent. In a further attempt to communicate my feelings, I touched my heart and then touched his chest, and then put my two hands together. In sign language, it meant, "I feel your heart—and your hurt."

At last I put down the flute. The boy reached for it. I said in Lakota, "Go ahead and try it." It was the first time I'd spoken and, of course, he looked at me in confusion. He spoke, but I did not understand his words either. I shrugged my shoulders and Mato Ska laughed aloud. Then he picked up my flute.

How to communicate with him when we speak different languages, I wondered? I thought of Sitting Bull and his drawings in the dirt and wondered if pictures could say the words for me. I picked up a stick and drew a person, and then another person. My people looked funny and White Bear laughed again, but he also nodded in understanding, pointing to indicate one boy for each of us. I drew small arms on my figures and then joined the hands together in friendship. He understood and nodded.

"*Kola,*" I said, the word for friend.

The boy looked at me and said a word in his language that I assumed meant 'friend.'

Friends.

I wanted so badly to tell the boy about my dream, why I had come, how I had proven myself a man by killing a buffalo and traveled far to reach him, but I knew this was far beyond what drawings in the dirt could say. Instead I pointed to the boy and said *Mato Ska*, or White Bear.

He did not understand my words, but understood that I was giving him a name. He said, "Matoshka," putting the syllables together, and laughing at himself for how it sounded. He said it again, more clearly this time. "*Mato Ska.*"

I drew a crude bear on the ground. There was no way to paint it white but the boy saw the figure and said, "Bear." I copied his sound and we both laughed at how odd my imitation of his language sounded. I pointed at the bear and said, "Mato."

Mato Ska then pointed at me, raised two fingers to his own eyes, and said, "Eyes."

I understood. The name he gave me came from the eyes he'd seen peeking out from behind the tree. I remembered the mud covering my face, and how it had frightened him to see only eyes in a mud-smeared face.

"*Ista.*" I said, the Lakota word for "eyes."

"*Eeshta,*" the boy repeated.

This first attempt at conversation excited me. I saw he was excited as well. I repeated the word *ista* and he said it more clearly.

I removed the rope from Mato Ska's neck, stood up, and went to the edge of the creek. He watched as I picked up a handful of mud, brought it back, sat down again, and smeared the mud gently on his neck.

"*Pejuta,*" I said in Lakota. Medicine. Grandmother had taught me about the healing properties of mud. Since we are raised from soil, she had said, wet soil is a good poultice. She'd also told me the roots of strong trees—the heart of the plant—contained good *pejuta,* for healing, but I didn't want to take the time to make a poultice of tree roots.

Mato Ska touched the mud on his neck and smiled, nodding approval, but he seemed more interested in learning additional words. He tried to repeat the word but did it poorly.

I said the word slowly, "*Pejuta.*" Then I picked up my drawing stick and said, "*Cha.*"

He repeated the word in Lakota, and then said "wood" in his own language. I mouthed the unfamiliar word, liking the way it felt on my tongue.

We had crossed a big barrier and were now learning to communicate, but I had no idea how to explain that I had come to rescue him, to take him back to my people. This was a puzzle I couldn't yet solve.

We exchanged many words this way. We picked up stones, touched trees and pointed at insects, exchanging the words from two languages and practicing the unfamiliar sounds. After nearly an hour of this word play, I heard thunder and noticed dark clouds gathering out in the western sky. A storm was moving fast in our direction.

I heard voices, the father again yelling at someone, and put my finger to my lips, signaling silence. I stood up and pointed toward the cabin, to myself, and then into the woods in the direction from which I had first emerged. I started to leave but Mato Ska stood up and took my arm, as if to keep me there. I shook my head to let him know it would not be good for the father to see me. I quickly waded the creek and took cover where I could still see the cabin.

The mother and brother were walking toward the creek, but the father came out and yelled at them. He pointed and grabbed the mother's arm roughly and pushed her back inside, calling for the other son to follow. I saw the powerful hesitation in the brother; the call of one twin to another was a strong call. Mato Ska's brother could not be comfortable with the way his twin was treated, but the father yelled and scowled and, with a final look toward Mato Ska, he went back into the cabin.

Both relieved and saddened, I realized the father meant to leave the boy out in the storm, to further punish him. We were safe, for now, but I could not understand the actions of this father. It angered me. I strode back across the creek, took Mato Ska's hand and pointed up toward the cliff where my horse was tethered—where the small cave waited to keep us dry. The wind whipped through the treetops.

I led Mato Ska up the hill. We gained the small shelter and I took the blanket off Wasaka and threw it over the branches I'd put above the shelter to give us additional protection from the rain. Mato Ska went in first and settled himself on my buffalo robe, grinning. I crawled in after, flattened my hands toward the dry roof, and smiled.

The storm broke. A cold rain fell in sheets across the land, but inside we were dry and warm. Mato Ska pointed to the flute. I picked it up and began to play. Every once in awhile I dropped the flute away from my lips and sang the verses of the song that seemed a part of this dream, this adventure. Mato Ska stretched out on the robe and put his head on the exposed fur. The cave was small—his feet nearly touched the far side—but it was big enough for the two of us.

Outside, the world was drenched in cold rain. I smelled forest and mud and lightning. The wind carried the smells into the cave and we each took a long breath. Mato Ska clearly preferred to take his father's punishment and be tied to a tree in order to be left alone with the bird and forest sounds.

We are alike this way, I thought. We are brothers, like Mato Ska and his twin are brothers. It seemed strange to think of myself as a brother to one so different, and yet my heart said it was so.

All during the storm I played the flute stopping only to sing my song. We were held in nature's hands; protected and sheltered as the rain washed the world, nourished the plants, slaked the thirst of animals and greedy streambeds. All of these thoughts I put into my flute and let them come out as music. When I looked at Mato Ska again, he was asleep.

I must have dozed also because, when I came back to myself, the storm had passed over. To the west, the orange glow of the sun returned as the rain dwindled to a light shower. I worried that the angry father, or the mother and brother, might soon be coming to check on Mato Ska. I shook his arm to wake him and pointed back down toward the creek. He shook his head, looking distressed.

How could I tell Mato Ska of my plans to take him north to my village? Rather than attempt it, I rose and pointed again down toward the creek and started walking. He stood in the entrance of the shelter still shaking his head. The father's thunder stick worried me. I ran toward the creek. My friend followed. I knew then that he would go willingly with me, but we needed a plan.

With a mixture of sign language, facial expressions, and lines scratched into the earth, I let him know I would be hiding and watching in the underbrush—that he should stay silent and not tell anyone I was there. I tied the rope once again around his neck. That rope—I wanted to toss it into the creek and watch it float away—but it was not yet time.

The silence was broken by voices and yelling coming from the cabin. I hastily erased my own tracks, placed a finger signaling silence across my mouth, and then crossed the creek to hide where I could still watch.

The mother and brother came down to the riverbank. I worried that Mato Ska would say something, or point in my direction, but he didn't. When they reached Mato Ska, they stopped and stared at him. He was not crying or afraid. He was smiling—and completely dry. The stronger brother said something and touched Mato Ska's clothes, touched the mud on his neck. I realized we'd made a terrible mistake. They had left him in the storm as punishment and now he was not afraid—and not wet.

I watched, wondering what would happen.

The strong brother sensed my presence, I was sure. He looked around, touched Mato Ska's neck again, and then turned his head directly toward me. My heart jumped, but I knew he could not see me. I was invisible. Then the father came out of the cabin. The strong brother grabbed Mato Ska, yanked the rope free, and hauled him to the river. He splashed water on Mato Ska's shirt and head, and hastily scrubbed his neck clean.

This brother is smart, I thought. He too wanted to protect Mato Ska from his father's wrath. In our shared need to protect, I realized this stronger brother was also *my* brother. It shocked me—to realize I took these two white boys as brothers so easily. How I wanted to make contact with this brother as well, to let him know I was taking Mato Ska with me. I worried that his family would think him dead, eaten by wolves or something, after we had gone.

When his father approached, Mato Ska hung his head and looked pitiful. I wanted to laugh at his clever play-acting. The father would never believe we had spent the storm playing the flute and watching the world be washed new. I wondered how much of Mato Ska's slow awkwardness was a game he played.

This father was like an angry bear, always yelling and growling at his wife and sons. He barked at Mato Ska and pointed toward the cabin. The family walked back up the slope with the father close behind. They disappeared into the cabin and, when they came back out, Mato Ska was now in dry clothes. The three went back to work on the stack of logs.

When they had worked a while, Mato Ska once again held himself down low and his father pointed toward the little building. I held my breath, waiting to see what would happen, but he emerged still dry on the front of his pants. His father looked him over and nodded, perhaps convinced the punishment of being left out in the storm had been effective.

Mato Ska looked my way many times but never said a word to his father or brother. I was safe.

Late in the day, when the sun had dropped in the western sky, the woman came out and called to the man and her sons and they again disappeared into the cabin. I realized they were probably eating their evening meal and preparing for bed. I'd have to wait until the next day to see Mato Ska—and to know what would happen then.

My own stomach grumbled. I had a burning curiosity to see the family at their meal, sitting together inside that cabin. I nearly crept up the slope to peek in the windows but resisted the urge—the memory of that thunder stick kept me away.

Cramped and tired from remaining still for so long, I finally went back to my shelter, ate some dried buffalo meat, and then led Wasaka down to the creek to drink. It had now been three days since I'd left the village. Soon Grandfather would send riders to look for me. I didn't want to endanger any of the men, but could not rush this task.

The time Mato Ska and I had spent together during the storm had been an opening. Now, in the dimming light of the day, it seemed a crazy thing. I was actually planning to steal Mato Ska from his family and bring him back to my village. What was I doing? And why? I decided to leave my actions in the hands of *Wakan Tanka*, to let him decide what was to unfold this day—or tomorrow. I would spend another night alone and see what the new day would bring. My body was bone tired. I stretched out and fell into a deep, dreamless sleep.

14 Mato Ska—Freeing the White Bear

Again I was startled awake by the shrieking, noisy bird I'd heard the day before, only this time I knew what it was. Looking out from the ridge toward the cabin, I saw the people were already awake. In fact, the father was angry and yelling again. His voice cut the air louder than the shriek of the bird as he roughly grabbed Mato Ska and hauled him to the woodpile.

Something had happened.

The man picked up a stick and began hitting Mato Ska on his backside. I felt every blow of that stick. My friend cried out, and it was all I could do not to cry out, too. This man was a violent, angry man who used his strength against those who were weaker. His anger, like a fever, spread through the air into my body. I shivered and trembled with anger.

The mother ran out of the cabin crying, screaming at the father. I knew she wanted him to stop but he did not stop. His anger was fierce. He threw the stick down and pushed Mato Ska toward the creek, still gesturing and hollering. Mato Ska stripped his clothes off and began scrubbing them in the sand and water on the edge of the creek. The sight of that pale, wounded skin on his back made me wince. I saw that he had not only wet himself, but had also soiled his clothing like a baby.

When the boy had cleaned himself as best he could and put on the soggy clothing again, his father shoved him to the ground, and tied him to the tree. He stomped off, still yelling.

I realized what he had done. Oh devious boy, I thought. Mato Ska scanned the trees where he knew I would be waiting and grinned. He pointed to his eyes and said, "Ista?"

It was then, in that moment, I realized that this white boy—this white bear—must have been waiting for me, just as I had been waiting to find the white bear tied to a tree. This strong action was meant to be.

With no more hesitation, I stepped out from behind the trees, crossed the creek, removed the rope and said "Come." Mato Ska nodded. He followed me across the creek and up the slope to the shelter. I gathered my belongings, packed them onto the back of Wasaka, and pointed for Mato Ska to get on the horse. He tried, but the recent whipping caused him too much pain. So, with complete understanding between us although neither of us could speak the other's language, we followed the stream and walked away from the log cabin—and the angry father.

15 The Journey Home

We walked until it was time to turn north again. Before we left the stream, I showed Mato Ska how to use the mud to soothe and heal his red, swollen backside. His clothing still stunk. I pinched my nose and grimaced. Mato Ska laughed and pointed at the leather clothing. I had no extra clothing with me so I gathered mint growing alongside the creek, mixed it with mud, and showed Mato Ska how to scrub the stink out of his clothing and off his body.

Later, while we rested, I used a stick to draw more pictures on the dirt. I drew a cabin with smoke coming out of the top; then, some distance away, I drew a tipi village with many people. I drew two figures and a long curving line from the cabin to the tipi village. I wanted to be sure Mato Ska understood we were making a journey away from his family. And that he agreed to go. He nodded, looking a little sad, but used his two fingers to walk the line away from the cabin and away from his mother and brother. Then he pointed to my flute and motioned for me to play.

I hesitated, wondering if we were being followed. We'd seen and heard nothing since leaving the creek so I played softly to welcome the day opening around us. Mato Ska smiled, his sorrows gone for the moment. I worried about Grandfather and how soon the search party would be dispatched to look for us. I was anxious to return to the village so the riders would not go as far as the cabin and the man with the thunder stick—and the missing son.

I packed the flute away and pointed north. We spent the next many hours walking beside Wasaka, or breaking into a run until we were panting, and then walking again. Mato Ska was slow and clumsy. He stumbled often, sometimes falling down. I looked at the chunky shoes and thought they looked too big for his feet. I did have a second pair of moccasins in my roll that I used when the weather was colder—they were lined in fur. His feet looked about the same size as mine so I handed them to him. He sat down, tried on the soft moccasins, and then jumped up and began singing and dancing until I was breathless from laughing at him. He took the chunky shoes and tossed them out onto the prairie, but I retrieved them, not wanting to leave such an obvious sign of our having passed this way.

Mato Ska pointed at my leather shirt, dancing the fringe with his finger, and then pointed at his own shirt. I did not have a second shirt, but he wanted to wear the leather one so we traded shirts. The fabric of Mato Ska's shirt felt fine and smooth. I didn't know how to close the front of it and fumbled with it until he laughed and helped me slide the buttons through the little holes.

I liked the feel of his shirt against my skin, and Mato Ska proudly patted the leather shirt he now wore. He pointed again and said something in his language. I said "shirt" in Lakota. Repeating the word carefully, Mato Ska then touched his feet, toes, knees . . . each time asking for the word, each time repeating it slowly.

For the rest of the long day of traveling, Mato Ska asked again and again for the Lakota words. I said them slowly. I realized that even if his feet did not always work together, my new brother was quick to learn language. He tasted every word on his tongue and seemed almost to eat them; he remembered the name for every object I named.

My moccasins appeared to make Mato Ska stumble less often, but he was still awkward. I showed him how to hold

116

on to Wasaka's mane and pace his own gait with the smooth gait of the horse. There was so much I wanted to teach him; about the connection between horse and man, about the connection between man and all of earth's creatures, but the language difference kept me repeating only simple words. It frustrated us both to be reduced to naming simple objects, drawing pictures in the dirt, or signing everything, but I knew at the rate he was going, we'd soon be able to communicate easily. I did, however, show Mato Ska how to listen to Wasaka's heartbeat by putting a hand on the horse's chest, and another on his chest to show the connection.

During the heat of the day, we came to another creek and stopped to water and cool Wasaka. I filled my hands with water and poured it over the horse's flanks and back. Mato Ska saw what I was doing and joined in. Wasaka, finally tired of the soaking, shook himself violently to let us know enough was enough. We got showered. I took the next handful of water and threw it up into Mato Ska's face. He looked startled at first, then laughed, filled his palms with water, and did the same to me. Soon, both of us had shed our shirts and were dipping in the creek, laughing and splashing like little children.

Then we tried mounting Wasaka. I sat in front with Mato Ska on the back. It still hurt his backside but he pointed ahead, ready to ride, and I knew we could not walk the entire distance.

All day I listened for riders, for sounds of Mato Ska's father or brother pursuing us. There was no sound, no sign of anybody. We were completely alone on this journey. We walked, rode, and ran beside Wasaka until nightfall . . . and beyond. I wanted to get back to the village. Walking so much slowed us down but I knew Mato Ska was not used to this kind of rigorous travel. Finally, we chose a small area ringed by pine trees and made camp. I quickly built a tiny fire but it was too dark to hunt for a rabbit or bird so we finished eating the dried meats my mother had packed. The meat was tough but tasted good.

Mato Ska looked exhausted, but happy. He pointed once again to the flute and said, "Play the flute," in Lakota. I grinned. My brother was already forming full thoughts in my language.

I pointed to my ears and said, "Listen." Before I played, I made him listen to all the night sounds, raising my finger each time I heard a new one. I wanted him to understand the flute was Grandmother Earth's voice—birds and crickets, wolves and frogs, the wind, all belonging to her. To demonstrate, I played a while, listened again until I heard a new sound, and then played it as closely as I could.

Mato Ska nodded and smiled. He understood. The fire crackled and all around us the night was rich with sound. He took the flute from me and put it to his lips. The first notes were more like a thing dying than the living things of Earth, and I laughed at him. But as he practiced and listened, he was soon imitating the voices of the night with the flute. I thought again that whatever *Wakan Tanka* had not given this boy in his awkward body—he'd given extra to his keen ears.

Before the sun had cracked the sky with its light, I was up and ready to ride, wanting to reach the village early that day. I gave Mato Ska a shake and he jumped up—a wild, frightened look on his face—his arms instantly covering his head in a defensive move as if fending off the blows of his father's stick. It took him several minutes to orient himself, to remember that he was no longer under his parents' roof but under a roof of stars and moon.

I flattened my palms and moved them side-to-side like smooth water to show him there was no reason to be afraid. I kicked dirt over the remaining embers from our fire and said, "Come, Mato Ska."

We quickly repacked the bedroll onto Wasaka's back and then walked up a hillside to watch the sun rise. We had been slowly climbing the day before and now we looked at the orange glow spreading over the lands we had journeyed through. The birds were in full song and the world was alive with light and music.

Mato Ska smiled and said, "Beautiful," in Lakota.

We spent the long morning practicing phrases like "I am hungry. I am tired. I have to relieve myself." I grinned at the last, pointing toward Mato Ska's midsection. He laughed and said, "Bad boy." I noticed this need to wet his pants had been left behind at the cabin where his father lived.

When Mato Ska learned more of our language, I would explain that someday we would return to see his family, but that we would take him back changed—no longer a clumsy boy, but a grown man. Although I could not yet explain any of this to him, my mind entertained itself with the images of Mato Ska a strong man and a strong hunter, riding back on his own horse, and his introduction of me to his brother and parents. I didn't know when that would be—only that it was a part of what we would do together.

16 Homecoming

Mato Ska's backside was healing and we rode now more than we walked. My thoughts turned toward the village and what would happen when I arrived bringing the white bear with me. How would the people treat him? Except for my father, my uncle and a few of the hunters, none had ever seen a white person. They had not had my dream. Would they welcome him? Would they treat him as a brother? Somehow, in preparing for this moment, these thoughts had never come to my mind.

I needn't have worried. Not only was the entire village waiting for me to return, they were waiting for me to return with Mato Ska. As we drew near, the same uncle I'd seen on my way out was again standing watch. "*Hoka He*," he called out when he saw us approach.

"Don't be afraid," I told Mato Ska, using the calm water sign again. "He is my uncle."

Mato Ska raised a hand high in the air and lifted his eyebrows.

I laughed. "Yes, a big man. A very big man. *Tatanka Wanagi* is his name. Buffalo Spirit," I said slowly. I had never thought about how imposing my uncle could be. He was strong and surefooted, taller than me by at least a foot. When he walked toward us, Mato Ska stayed close to my side.

Tatanka Wanagi said, "Your father wanted to come looking for you yesterday. He had already gathered a search

121

party, but your Grandfather stopped him—said he sensed you were on your way home. They are waiting for you. And for you." He smiled at my friend.

"Uncle, this is Mato Ska, the boy I dreamed about."

Uncle offered his hand. When Mato Ska stretched his hand out to meet it, my uncle slid his own hand up toward the elbow. This greatly eased my fear of the welcome he would receive. This special handshake was reserved for close family members—not for strangers.

Mato Ska said, "Greetings, *Kola,*" in Lakota.

Tatanka Wanagi's eyes widened and he laughed. "Leave your horse with me. I'll rub him down and water him. Your grandfather waits. Take your pack and go."

I thanked Uncle and together Mato Ska and I walked toward the camp. A group of children playing on the edge of the village spotted us and ran ahead calling out to the others to come and see. By the time we entered, all the people had gathered to greet us. There was much laughter and hugging and handshakes. I had forgotten we were still wearing each other's shirts until the younger children started laughing and pointing and asking who was who. I joined their game by introducing myself as Mato Ska, and Mato Ska as Little Chief. The children circled Mato Ska and hugged him and called out to him, "Little Chief, so good to see you, so glad you came back safe."

It was a great game. I saw Mato Ska was moved almost to tears by the greeting he'd received. When my father and mother came up, Father looked at Mato Ska and said, "Greetings, my son."

This was a fine moment for me, that Father would accept my actions and publicly welcome Mato Ska among us as his son.

I introduced my mother, Morning Star, and she hugged us both and promised us a good meal soon. "You must be hungry."

Mato Ska smiled and said in clear, slow Lakota, "I am hungry."

Charging Bull laughed and said, "This is good. You teach him our words. But you will eat later. First, your Grandfather is waiting in his tipi. Go speak with him."

We went immediately to Grandfather's tipi and asked to enter.

"Yes, yes . . . come in. I have been waiting."

We bent down and entered. I watched Mato Ska's eyes go as wide as round stones when he stared at the cozy interior of the tipi. The floor was covered with soft robes, the sides hung with tools, pipes, leather bags, and other things. Grandfather sat on one of the robes watching Mato Ska.

I felt proud as my white bear went over to Grandfather, kneeled down and said, again in slow, clear Lakota, "Greetings, my grandfather."

Grandfather said nothing for a long moment, only gazed at Mato Ska. I imagined him thinking of his own dreams, of the changes coming at the hands of this boy's people, a hard thing to have seen. Finally he nodded, the corners of his mouth lifting slightly, and said to me, "Already you teach him our kinship ways, our Lakota ways." He nodded. "It is good. Welcome, *Takoja*." He reached out and touched Mato Ska's head, and said to me, "Now, you must tell me all about this journey you have taken."

I told Grandfather everything that had happened since I'd left camp several days earlier. I spoke rapidly and Grandfather interrupted several times to ask for more details. Mato Ska said nothing, just listened, obviously fascinated to hear the language in full sentences and speeches. I imagined his ears soaking up the Lakota language much as moss absorbs rain. And it was the first time I saw that my curiosity was like Grandfather's; he wanted to know every detail of our journey.

Finally, after I had told him all I could remember, Grandfather said, "There is something different about this boy. Tell me."

"He is a twin, Grandfather. He has a brother who looks exactly like him, but the brother is strong and sure-footed. Mato Ska is. . . I don't know . . . he is awkward, not so strong, but he is smart. He learns our words quickly." I explained how Mato Ska was purposely wetting himself, angering his father so he could be near the creek.

Grandfather nodded. "A twin. Yes, often when twins are the same in their bodies, they are not the same in their spirits. And because you dreamed of this boy, you are also like a twin to him. Interesting. And what does *Wakan Tanka* have in mind for you both?"

I wondered the same. "I think it is part of your dream also, Grandfather. I want to teach Mato Ska about our ways, how we live. I want to stop what is coming."

Grandfather looked sad. "No, Grandson. I have told you before that what is coming is too big for you to stop. But there is meaning in everything, and I think you are right in what you have done. You will teach this boy our ways, the ways of the Lakota people, and someday he will return to his people and teach them. Go now, and introduce your brother to the grandmothers and the people. Sometime soon, we will go someplace that I want to show both of you, but it will be a long journey. First you must rest and let Mato Ska get used to being in this new place. He learns words easily."

"Yes, he does."

As if Mato Ska understood what we were talking about, he pulled one of the buffalo robes aside, took a stick from near the fire pit and drew on the earth. He drew one figure alone and said, "Mato Ska." Then he drew a multitude of straight lines and waved a hand to indicate the people of our village. Finally, he erased the single lone figure and added it to the middle of the people.

Grandfather understood. "I think he says he wants to be here with the people and that he is grateful."

I nodded and laughed. "We have drawn a lot of pictures these past few days. We've gotten pretty good at it."

The evening passed in a blur. We ate with my parents, spent the evening meeting and greeting my people, playing with the children, introducing Mato Ska to my little brother. Mato Ska was not afraid to try speaking words, even when the children laughed and joked about his pronunciation. They simply corrected him, speaking slowly, and he carefully repeated each word back to them.

In the frenzy of activity, I noticed the only person who did not come to meet Mato Ska was my cousin, Rabbit. I worried about this, that Rabbit would feel himself displaced by my new friend. I sought him out and found him sitting on my stony perch above the village, watching the actions below just as I had done so often. When I approached, he would not look at me. "I am back," I said.

"I see this is so," he said.

"Will you come and meet him?" There was no need for further identification. Rabbit knew I was talking about the white boy. He continued to look down at the village— not at me. I didn't know what else to say so I left him there alone and walked back down, a bit hurt and angry.

Rabbit had been the only person in the village who refused to greet Mato Ska.

As the sun rapidly dropped in the sky, I took Mato Ska to Grandmother's tipi. This grandmother was my mother's mother. She was a great healer and attended nearly every birth in the camp. I introduced her simply as *Unci*, our Lakota word for Grandmother. Mato Ska spoke the word respectfully.

Unci was a small woman with no extra flesh on her body. Her hair had long ago gone white and I had loved her smile for as long as I could remember. She was a gentle spirit and greeted Mato Ska with a warm hug. He seemed instantly absorbed into the sphere of her warmth. He plopped down beside her as if he might never leave again.

She had lost her husband three winters earlier and now lived alone in her tipi. The poles of the tipi were hung with plants, leaves, and bags of roots; the air was tinged with the smell of mint, licorice root, and a musky, mushroom scent. Again, the fire pit was circled with soft buffalo robes and hides.

Unci liked to talk. She was a great talker and seemed not to notice or care that Mato Ska did not understand her ramblings. When she saw his neck, she immediately began preparing a healing poultice, taking down several different roots, grinding them in a stone bowl, and mashing them into a muddy mixture. She talked all the while, explaining what she was doing and why—how the roots carry the healing properties of Grandmother Earth. He listened to every word, nodding and smiling. I felt invisible, as if they alone were in the tipi. When the poultice was prepared, she smeared the thick mixture on his neck and made soothing, singing noises as she did so.

"Tomorrow I will clean this off and prepare a second poultice," Unci said. She patted his shirt and then pointed at my shirt and said to Mato Ska, "Little Chief is your brother now. He will give you anything you need. He is a good boy. Brothers take care of each other." She rummaged in a corner of the tipi and brought out a pale new leather shirt, fringed and adorned with beautiful quillwork. "And I will take care of Little Chief. Here, a shirt I have just finished. I give it to you." She fumbled with the awkward buttons of the odd shirt I wore, helping me take it off and put the new one on.

The new leather shirt was soft, scraped smooth by her hands. I was touched by her gift. "Thank you, Unci. It is the most beautiful shirt I have ever worn."

"Yes. It looks good on you too. You are nearly a man, Little Chief. I did not notice." She pointed to Mato Ska. "Come back tomorrow night and I will wash and repaint his neck." She picked up the discarded cloth shirt. "This one I will keep, to make something nice."

When we left, she was fingering the unfamiliar cloth, her eyes keen and thoughtful, watching Mato Ska. I knew the shirt would soon be a multitude of small bags holding Unci's unguents and herbs.

17 *Lakota Oyate* in Winter

That was Mato Ska's entry into my village. For many days after, my father posted extra men to watch the prairie for signs of unfamiliar riders. Nobody ever came looking for Mato Ska and eventually the extra watch was abandoned.

Autumn came and with it the colder nights and occasional bitter winds that forewarned of winter. Mato Ska and I settled into a routine of helping to prepare the village for the cold season. He was not yet good on a horse, and had no horse of his own, so he stayed in the village with Unci when I went with the experienced hunters. I wondered if he missed his brother or the cabin with the smoke curling from the chimney, or his parents, but he never complained. Often he sought me out in the evenings to hear my flute, or Grandfather would take my white brother into his tipi to ask him more questions. My elder's thirst for understanding of Mato Ska's people was great.

With every passing moon, he gained more and more of the language. He seemed content with the dramatic change in his life, and the villagers soon became accustomed to him helping Unci gather her fall plants, berries, and roots. I saw that she and Mato Ska had become close friends, and it pleased me.

When the weather turned, and winter had definitely arrived, it did not surprise anybody when Unci approached my mother and father with the request to let Mato Ska spend the winter in her tipi. She was alone and Charging Bull's tipi was full. He could tend her fire and help prepare her medicines. I was sorry to have him leave my parents' tipi. I had envisioned myself teaching the white bear our Lakota ways, but he was entranced with Unci and her healing plants; hungry to learn more of Lakota healing. And the people of the village were teaching him about living life as a Lakota man.

It was all being done without much help from me.

One bright, brittle day when the pine needles and branches were shimmering from an ice storm, Rabbit came to our tipi. He handed me a flute he'd made with the help of his father. The craftsmanship was beautiful, there were small bears carved into its sides as if they were chasing one another. The wood was pale ash. I looked at the flute and then at Rabbit. "The carving is amazing."

"Thanks. It is for Mato Ska. Will you give it to him?"

I knew this gift was a peace offering—Rabbit's way of making up for having ignored Mato Ska when he first came to the village. "Come," I said, "You can give it to him yourself."

His offering closed the rift I'd felt between us since I had killed a buffalo and he had not. He followed me to Unci's tipi. Mato Ska was outside tending the cooking fire. Rabbit handed him the flute and said, "I made this for you."

Mato Ska had not been aware of the strain between us although I'd told him of the first time Rabbit and I left the village in search of him. Now, he took the flute as if it were a rare and fragile plant. His eyes watered as he traced the fine raised figures of the bears chasing one another up the flute. "I don't believe this. It is for me?"

Rabbit said, "Yes, to welcome you to our village. I know you like the flute."

Mato Ska raised it to his lips and blew a note as clear and shining as the ice on the pines. He looked at Rabbit and said, "I will treasure this as my finest possession. Will you teach me to carve like this?"

Rabbit looked surprised and touched by Mato Ska's response to his gift. "I can do that."

In the cold of winter, the ice between Rabbit and me thawed at last. I was glad and noticed over the coming weeks that Mato Ska spent a lot of time with Rabbit learning to whittle wood into small figures. It amazed me once again that the boy's awkward body covered such a keen mind, such skilled fingers.

Night after night the soft musical tones of the flute lifted from Unci's tipi. The sound was beautiful—and lonely. I knew Mato Ska was missing his brother, his twin. I thought of the sadness we must have caused his poor mother, left behind to deal with her husband's great anger. What, I wondered, would cause a man to be so angry?

I also knew that when it was time, I would take Mato Ska home again.

The winter was mild. Only three times did fierce winds and blowing snow drive the people into the tipis for several days where we all hunkered down to stay warm and safe. I spent these frigid days in Unci's tipi playing the flute with Mato Ska, and watching my white brother learn the healing arts. There were many fevers and coughs, and often he and Unci would go out into the cold to tend someone.

Unci enjoyed conversation and Mato Ska's language skills improved daily that winter.

I was amazed at how well they could converse. I thought back to the time by the creek when I'd had only my flute to communicate with him.

Under her care and teaching, he also seemed to grow taller, his feet more sure on the earth. Perhaps, I thought, this good care was all he needed to overcome whatever disability had followed him into life; good care and high regard from an Elder.

One day, as winter turned toward spring and the breezes began to come from the west instead of the bitter north, Mato Ska caught up with me on my way to hunt small game. "Can we talk, Little Chief?"

"Of course. Let's climb the hill and sit. We can talk there."

As we climbed, I again noticed my brother's surefootedness. Gone was the awkward gait, the clumsy falls. "You have grown stronger, Mato Ska, since you came to live with us."

"I have. Sometimes it feels as if I have never lived anywhere but here, Little Chief. But I did."

We gained the granite boulder where I liked to watch the village. "Yes, you did. Are you thinking about your family?"

"It's a strange thing, Little Chief. This feels like my family now, but sometimes I feel my brother late at night wondering and wondering what became of me. His spirit calls me. And I feel my mother must be sad at not knowing what happened to me."

"And what of your father?"

Mato Ska picked up a hard stone and rolled it in his hands, searching for the right words. "To judge my father would be easy. He can be hard, cruel even. But there is much you don't know about him. He was a colonel in the army—it changed him. Still, there is much I don't know. He was born on a ship coming to this country from Germany. My mother is Irish. They lost all connection with their families in those other lands. My father worked when he was just a boy, his family struggling to make it in this new land. Your people have been on this land for so long. Your time is unchanged, Little Chief. I think we don't know what my father's spirit contains."

I smiled. "You speak well, friend. All those words in just one season. Amazing."

Mato Ska laughed. "It's Unci; she never stops talking. I had to learn to speak—or spend my winter listening only."

He tossed the stone down and said, "I want to go to see my family when winter has passed."

"I thought as much," I said. "We should go talk to Grandfather. See what he thinks."

After the evening meal, I sought out Mato Ska and pointed toward Grandfather's tipi. We went together and asked to be let in. He opened the flap and said, "Come in, Grandsons."

When we were seated inside the tipi, Mato Ska asked, "How is your cough, Grandfather?"

"It is better. I think I will see yet another spring."

I looked from one to the other. I had not realized Grandfather had been sick. Mato Ska took a small pouch and handed it to the old man. "I made this for you, to soothe your throat."

Yes, I thought, this white bear had made a home among us in just a few short months. I said, "Grandfather, Mato Ska wants to go visit his family and let them know he is alive and well."

Grandfather considered this for a long time and then addressed his words to Mato Ska. "It is not yet time. When Little Chief wanted to come for you, there were many things he had to do before I would let him go. He needed a strong horse. You need a strong horse. He needed to train with the men. You have trained only with your grandmother."

"But Grandfather . . . ." Mato Ska began.

"Tshhh." Grandfather hushed him before he could speak further. "You have learned much, Mato Ska, but there is yet much to learn." He smiled. "And you are a very bad rider."

Mato Ska looked stunned and hurt at his words. The expression on his face made me laugh. I remembered too well how Grandfather used words, like a sharp stick, to get his point across.

"He has no horse yet, Grandfather," I said.

"Exactly. So that is the first order. There is something I have been wanting to show you both, a special place. We will travel together to this place and, on the way, perhaps we will get Mato Ska a horse as well."

"When?" I asked.

"Tomorrow."

Mato Ska seemed to quickly forget the comment about being a bad rider and said, "But Grandfather, your cough. Perhaps you should wait for a few more days to travel."

"No, I will be fine. Besides, I will have you with me. You can tend me."

I said, "Good. We will come to your tipi early in the morning and bring your horse.

Grandfather smiled, a gleam in his eye. "I will awaken you. It has been a long time since either of you rose before me."

18 The Place Where Twins Come From

Early the next morning I heard a voice singing. It blended with my dream. In the dream I was living life in a far distant future as an older man. My house was made of metal, webbed around me, hot and sticky, and nothing outside my door looked familiar. It was a strange dream, both heavy and light. Finally, the sound of Grandfather singing softly outside the tipi reached my ears and my mind cleared of the night dream. I got up and went outside. I washed quickly and got ready to go on the journey with Grandfather. Mato Ska came out at the same time. The sky was a pale pink when we arrived at Grandfather's tipi.

I said, "I'll get your horse, Grandfather."

"No," he said, "Take your packs and mine, and we'll go to the horses. Time for Mato Ska's first lesson."

When we reached the edge of the small valley where the horses grazed, Grandfather made a small sound and his horse raised its head. It cut away from the herd and came directly to him. I did as Grandfather had and made my special call. Wasaka came to me.

Grandfather said to Mato Ska, "Your horse is part of you—he will help keep you out of danger. We have trained them to know our signal. You will soon have your own horse to train."

The day's ride would be too long for Mato Ska to ride behind me so we chose a gentle mare from the herd for him to ride until he had his own.

Grandfather, Mato Ska, and I rode until late afternoon. It was a pleasant day, balmy and warm with no hint of the recent winter winds. As far as we looked in any direction, we saw no signs of people. We were alone on the big land. Finally Grandfather said, "Here. We will make camp here."

We stood on a small, pine-studded ridge overlooking a flowing prairie. In the distance a lone mountain sat. Grandfather pointed to it and said, "This is what I wanted to show both of you. It is called *Mato Paha*, Bear Mountain. You have been here before, Little Chief, when you were very young. It is a sacred mountain and we come here to pray. If you look, you will see a bear on its side."

Mato Ska and I immediately saw the shape now that Grandfather had named it.

"Now, look again." He turned to me and said, "Look carefully and you will see another shape."

I let my eyes relax as I had been taught, to take in not just what was in front of me, but also the finer movements and details in the surrounding environment. This way I saw the mountain—but I saw the mountain in relationship to the sky and land around it. Slowly, the shape of the bear changed and became something different. "A woman. I see a woman who is pregnant. She is lying on her back."

Grandfather laughed. "Good Grandson. You got it. Mato Ska, do you see it?"

"Yes, Grandfather."

"They say this mountain is where all twins come from. I have been thinking about this mountain since you told me Mato Ska has a twin brother. Twins are very powerful; they are hooked together and share each other's thoughts and feelings. When you told me about your dream the first time, about the white bear tied to a tree and how you needed to rescue him, I wondered and wondered what it could mean. And then you brought him here, said you wanted to teach him our ways, to give him understanding about our Lakota people so he could return and tell his own people about us. I am coming to understand your dream, Little Chief . . . and my own."

I sensed the connection, but could not make it become clear in my mind. "I don't yet see how it is all connected, Grandfather."

Mato Ska had been listening intently. "I think I understand, Little Chief."

"You do? Tell me what you understand," I said.

"I am a twin. When you took me with you, you took my brother as well. How could it be otherwise? So when I learn, he learns. And that mountain is my mother. My brother and I were born from her. There is also the connection to the bear. You call me White Bear."

I felt as if I'd missed something important. Grandfather and Mato Ska were staring at each other, some communication passing between them I could not understand. I shook my head, laughed, and said to Mato Ska, "I thought *Wakan Tanka* gave me the dream to teach you about our ways. But the village has taught you. Grandfather has taught you. Unci has taught you. I only brought you to them."

Grandfather nodded. "Yes, that is always the way of dreams. It is never one person alone who is dreaming but a larger dreaming. Dreams come from the other realms."

Shivers ran along my arms and legs. I'd not felt that for a while, since before I rescued Mato Ska. I thought of my dream of the white bear, and my dream just the night before of a man living in an unfamiliar world, webbed in metal. And I thought of this mountain. Grandfather said it was sacred, that it linked the realms. Perhaps it links time as well, an intersection between what is now—and what is yet to come.

I could not grasp it all, not with my mind, but I felt its truth. Somehow my spirit had lodged itself between twin

137

brothers and separated them. I didn't yet know what the full import of this would be.

Or what terrible consequences would come to me as a result of it.

Grandfather interrupted my philosophical thoughts with more practical matters. "Let's eat. When we have set our camp, we will ride over to the sacred mountain and offer our prayers to the place where all twins come from, where all worlds meet. We will ask *Wakan Tanka* for guidance and help."

I felt caught in a cloud, my thoughts thin and wispy. I set up our camp, ate supper, and then the three of us rode across the grassy plain to the base of the mountain. We tethered our horses and walked up the gentle slope. Grandfather prayed. Mato Ska and I took out our flutes and played with the wind and birds. We played together as we had never done before, tangling the tones and voices, stopping to sing the song that had come to me before I'd found the white bear. As we played, a pair of eagles flew high above, circling and circling as if sending strength and blessings our way. Grandfather pointed at the two male eagles and said, "Twins."

Later, when we had returned to camp and built a small fire to warm us against the chilly night, Grandfather said, "Tomorrow we will find a horse for Mato Ska."

Half teasing and half serious, I said, "I don't want to tangle with that stallion, Grandfather. He is big and mean, and will stop at nothing to protect his herd."

He tossed a chunk of wood into the fire and smiled. "We won't need to mess with that one. He cuts all the other studs out and they form their own herds. We will go for one of the other herds."

"Did Sitting Bull tell you where to find the horses?"

"Yes, he did."

I worried about my lack of experience, and Grandfather was too old to capture and train a horse. "Grandfather, what if we don't find them?"

He snorted. "Be *wasaka* Little Chief. Be strong. We have traveled. We have prayed for strength. Don't give up too easily. We stay until we find and catch a horse."

I was ashamed of my weak thoughts. I felt small again, like a boy who had just been scolded. I resolved to be strong and to do this thing we had set out to do.

Morning came quickly. I heard Grandfather coughing, trying to catch his breath, and it worried me. Mato Ska heard it also and took a mixture of plants and roots and dropped some on the still smoldering embers of the fire. The medicinal smoke soothed Grandfather's cough and he patted Mato Ska on the shoulder, "You have been a good student, I think. Now we shall see how good you are at catching a horse."

We headed east and, out of respect for Grandfather, set an easy pace. All morning and well into the afternoon, we rode up slight hills and down into valleys. We talked and sang as we rode. Mato Ska made up stories about the hills, giving each one a name and making them into funny characters. He had a tiny war going between Skunk Mountain and Red Fox Mountain, with the skunk winning. Grandfather laughed so hard he ended up in a coughing fit, but Mato Ska said this coughing was good—it was getting the bad stuff out of Grandfather's chest and making it clear again.

As the afternoon light waned, the horses began to act skittish, dancing left and right and raising their ears. Grandfather said, "We are getting close. The horses know there are other horses nearby."

When we topped the next ridge we saw a small herd of horses down below in a grassy bowl. I saw no giant white stallion and was relieved. It was one of the smaller herds.

Grandfather explained the plan. We would make camp just west of the herd and prepare a small enclosure in the gully using branches and downed trees. Then, in the morning, I was to ride farther east and get on the other side of the herd and chase them west toward the corral. When the horses came close, Mato Ska would release his borrowed mare and Grandfather's horse into the herd. The tamed horses would lead the others to the food and water we would have waiting. Then Mato Ska would choose his horse and we would release the others. The plan was set.

We made camp, built another small fire, and Mato Ska took his bow and arrow and proudly reappeared from the underbrush with a rabbit for our supper.

The scent of cooking meat soon filled the air. I was hungry, but when the meat was cooked, I noticed Grandfather ate very little and was coughing again. "Are you all right?" I asked.

"Yes, I will be fine, Grandson. But there is more I want to tell both of you. Finish eating and we will talk."

We finished the meat and Mato Ska carried the bones and scraps far from the camp for the small animals to carry off. When he returned, he took a place beside me, across the fire from Grandfather.

Again, I felt caught in cloud and wind. Grandfather talked and talked, his thoughts like a small dog following its nose. He talked about the changes he'd seen in his dreams, about the spider web, about Mato Ska's people coming, many people, and how the Lakota would be scattered to the four winds. Then he talked about how all things are measured in seven generations, that seven generations after this great change, there would be another great change.

He looked at Mato Ska and said, "You are only a boy, but you also will affect the seven generations. Bring your words to your people, Grandson. Tell the stories to your children and grandchildren. It is all part of the plan."

Mato Ska said nothing. Sadness seemed to hang over him like smoke, or dark clouds, and I wondered what my brother thought of such prophecy—that because of his people, the Lakota people he loved would be scattered.

Grandfather talked until both of us had curled up in our robes and covered ourselves against the night air.

The next morning, the plan went exactly as Grandfather had spoken it. I rode hard and chased the herd west. Mato Ska met me and released Grandfather's horse and his own into the herd. When the wild horses followed, Grandfather signaled his horse to come. The herd galloped into the roughly-made corral. It took only seconds for Mato Ska to choose his horse or, I thought, perhaps the horse chose him. It was a large, gleaming black stallion with a patch of white above its eyes. With some maneuvering, we released the rest of the herd and kept only the stallion in the corral with Wasaka and the other two horses for company.

Grandfather slapped me on the shoulder and said, "You did it, Grandson. Good work."

I said, "No, Grandfather. You did it."

"*Hiya*. I am an old man. I did nothing. But now you and Mato Ska must train this horse. You have seen it done and I will not be needed. I am tired. I want to go back to the village. I will leave you boys to tame the black stallion."

Before leaving, he went to Mato Ska and said, "You have chosen a good horse. Now you must come to know him. And he you."

Mato Ska looked disheartened. "You should stay, Grandfather."

"No, I can't. You and Little Chief will do well together. We are less than a day's ride from the village and I will be fine. Train your horse and then, when it is the right time, you can go see your brother again."

Before he left, he hugged me and said, "You are a fine grandson, Little Chief. You have made me proud today."

We watched Grandfather ride away until he was just a moving speck on the prairie. A heaviness settled over the exciting day. I asked, "Will he get well, Mato Ska?"

"Yes, for now. But his body is tired. And I think his dreams do not help."

19 *Eyakpakpa*—Flashing Horse

Taming and training the shining stallion took four days. Each day was charged with the high spirits of the horse, but also tinged with the sadness I felt at the thought of Grandfather some day passing into the spirit world. I could not imagine my life, or the village, without him.

Mato Ska did well. He undertook the training of the horse himself once he was clear on how to do it. I didn't have much to do so I spent long hours walking the bluffs and rubbing down Wasaka, not only to give comfort, but also to take comfort from him. I knew Mato Ska thought more and more of his twin.

We had talked about it the first night we were alone. He wondered when the right time would be to travel back to his home. As we sat watching the small curl of smoke rise up from our tiny flame, Mato Ska said, "His name is James . . . my brother."

I tried the name on my tongue. "And what is your name, Mato Ska?" How odd—that I had never asked his given name before this.

"My name is Jonathan."

I tried out his name on my tongue. It sounded more like "Ja-not-ton."

White Bear laughed and repeated it more slowly, stressing the first sound, and showing me how to put my tongue between my teeth to make the strange and unfamiliar 'th' sound. "Jonathan," I tried again.

"Better, my brother. But I like Mato Ska. I'm white—and still lumber along like a bear—it fits."

Later, as we lay beneath the night sky waiting for sleep to come, I said, "When your horse knows you better, we will go and check on your family. Soon."

"It must be soon, Little Chief. I feel something here," he pointed to his heart. "There is something going on with my brother. He may need me. We have always felt each other. Something is wrong."

"Your brother is probably looking for you. If you feel each other this way, he must know you are still alive and safe. When we get back, we will talk to Grandfather and make a plan. Have you thought about how you will approach your family? Will you go home to stay?"

"I don't want to, Little Chief. This life has been a different life for me, a good life. Thinking about living with my father again scares me. I am stronger, but not strong enough to stand up to him. My father doesn't like me. I disappoint him."

I turned and looked at him staring out at the night sky, the questions of his mind heavy on his heart. "Grandfather would say to give your worries to *Wakan Tanka*, to pray for the right answer. There is great power out there, Mato Ska." I pointed to the stars. "You see how each star is placed? There is order, just as there is order on the earth, in the waters, the trees, the plants. *Wakan Tanka* is never confused about where things belong. He knows. And he will tell us when we pray and ask him to reveal these things to us." I said, "I'll show you something."

I got up and found a smooth, solid stick and a fallen tree trunk. I rolled the hollow trunk into our camp. Mato Ska sat up, watching me. I hit the log and a rounded, solid sound went out into the surrounding trees. I began singing the song I'd caught the first time I'd gone to rescue the white bear. When I finished the song I told him, "The drum beat is the heartbeat of *Unci Maka*, of Grandmother Earth—it connects us to her heartbeat. When we sing and drum, we are talking with *Wakan Tanka*, and with our Grandmother. Put your concerns for your brother and mother into your mind and then sing with me. You'll see what I am saying."

We sang and prayed and thumped the hollow log until the moon rose high in the sky and it was time to sleep.

I was happy to have the four days of training Mato Ska's horse with nobody else around. He had spent so much time learning from Grandmother and the other women that it felt good to have him to myself. I taught him how to choose a whistle or bird sound to call his horse before offering the food and water. He chose a high-pitched whistle that could have been made by his flute.

When we were not working with his horse, we worked with our bows and arrows. Mato Ska was not much good with a bow. We laughed as he struggled to pull it back only to have the arrow fumble and hit the ground. I began shooting my arrows into the air and having him shoot after me to see if he could follow the arc of my arrow. It was a difficult task with much searching afterwards for the lost arrows, but his shooting improved with practice.

I found a deep pool of water with a beautiful little waterfall coming down a rocky slope and filling the pool. I shed my shirt and dove in, yelling for Mato Ska to join me.

He approached the bank and stared down at me. "I don't know how to swim," he admitted.

"What—a bear that can't swim? Come in and I will teach you."

"Is it cold."

I splashed him and shouted, "No, it is as warm as the water that flows by your brother's cabin."

"It is not my brother's cabin. It is my father's."

With a few strokes, I swam to the bank and looked up at him. "All the more reason to get in and learn," I challenged him.

The shirt was perhaps easier to shed than the old memories of his father's beatings, but soon he was naked and plopped into the water like an old, skinny bear. I laughed when he went under and came up sputtering and shaking. It was still icy cold from the spring runoff and he shivered.

"You do not speak the truth, Little Chief. This water is ice, all ice."

"Yes. Sure to toughen you up, girlie boy."

We spent several hours swimming, coming out frequently to warm up, only to dive back in again. I taught Mato Ska how to use his upper body and feet to keep his head above water. He had little strength in his upper body and his thin, white arms seemed to grab at the water instead of pushing it. Near the edge of the pool a branch hung over the water and I showed him how to use the branch to pull his body out of the water again and again. "This will strengthen your arms. You can use any branch. Pull up and hold your own weight until your muscles call out to you, until they shake, and then release. Do it again and again."

When we left the pool to return to the horses, Mato Ska wanted to race. He shoved me and took off to get a head start. I was a stronger runner and so I paced myself, staying alongside him until we got within a hundred paces of the corral, then I sprinted ahead, easily leaving him behind.

We spent the bright days climbing, running, swimming, and working with the black stallion. And we laughed a lot.

By the third day, the new horse was running when Mato Ska whistled. He was now able to rub his head and sides, to offer him food and water. The stallion was hungry and not as nervous.

"He is getting used to you." I said. "Have you thought of a name for him?"

"Not yet. I think it will come to me after I ride him the first time."

On the fourth day, we did as my father and the other hunters had shown me. We put the dark stallion between our two horses and rode into the pool of water. Mato Ska got off and swam around all the horses, staying close to his horse, rubbing him and talking calmly, sliding up the other horse and getting off, and then sliding onto the stallion's back and getting off. The churning water was not as great as when we trained the others, but it made our blood race anyway. When he had slid on and off his horse several times, I cried, "Now, Mato Ska. Ride him out now."

He got on the back of the stallion and rode him out of the water. I was close behind on Wasaka and we cleared the bank, broke into a brisk run, and ran to the edge of the meadow before turning and racing back to our camp. His face was bright with victory. "I did it, Little Chief." And then he leaned over and rubbed his horse's head and whispered, "We did it."

The stallion glistened in the sunlight, his wet hide taking the sunlight and flashing it back out into the world. "What is a Lakota word for something that shines in the sunlight?" Mato Ska asked.

"*Eyakpakpa.* Flashing," I said.

He tried the name on his lips. "*Eyakpakpa.*" Then he smiled. "That is my horse's name. Eyakpakpa."

"It is a good name, Mato Ska." His golden hair was wet and flashing also. They looked good together, man and horse, one light, one dark. "You already look like one beast instead of two, although your horse is far more handsome."

Early that afternoon, we packed our belongings onto the horses and rode back to the village. We were greeted by happy cries when Mato Ska rode in on his own horse. Grandmother said to come to her tipi when we had unpacked; that she and the other grandmothers had gifts for us, to celebrate.

Mato Ska got off Eyakpakpa and was instantly surrounded by children. They liked White Bear—and he liked them. We put our horses with the herd and he stayed awhile, stroking and whispering to his horse until it was no longer nervous. Calming people or animals seemed to come naturally to him.

When we went to Grandmother's tipi, several women had already gathered outside. They greeted Mato Ska and me with smiles and hugs.

Grandmother said, "The women want to honor both of you for getting a horse for Mato Ska. We have gifts."

The women gave us each a new pair of moccasins, the leather soft and yellow and adorned with intricate patterns of quillwork. They also had a set of leggings and a new shirt for each of us. Mato Ska stared at the beautiful clothing, his eyes wet with tears of gratitude. "What do we do with the old ones?"

The grandmothers laughed. "You keep them for times when you need extra, foolish boy," Unci said.

We stepped into the tipi to dress in our new clothing. My shirt was cut from white buckskin, as beautiful as new fallen snow, and Mato Ska's was a rich brown, the color of Lakota skin. I thought they had gotten us mixed up, that Mato Ska should have the white, and I the brown, but when we were dressed and staring at each other, I realized it was exactly right. Mato Ska and I were mixed up together, destined to be brothers in all ways, including the color of our skins. When we left the tipi, nearly all the people had gathered to see us in our new clothes. There was much cheering and celebrating. Again the little ones gathered around Mato Ska to touch the soft skin of his new shirt and exclaim over it.

Grandfather watched from the edge of the crowd. When the people were finished admiring the new clothes, he asked us to come to his tipi. "I too have gifts for you."

Inside, Grandfather reached behind a bundle and pulled out his own bow and quiver of arrows. He handed them to Mato Ska. "I am an old man. I will not hunt the buffalo again so I want to give you this. It is a good, strong bow and has served me well."

Mato Ska kept his arms at his sides and shook his head. "I have taken too many gifts today, sir. How can I take another?"

"What is this word, *sir?*" asked Grandfather.

"It is a word in my language, a word of respect for authority, for the one who is in charge."

Grandfather laughed. "How long have you lived with us, Mato Ska?"

He thought a moment. "It is coming up on one full year, Grandfather."

"I thought perhaps in such a long time you would have realized that Lakota people do not have one who is in charge. We do not have this word, *sir,* in our language. All are worthy of respect. Only *Wakan Tanka* is *sir.*"

Grandfather explained that the goods and property of the village only had value when they were circulated, when they traveled between people according to who needed what. "We take care of each other, Mato Ska. It is Lakota law."

"Yes, Grandfather. Then I will accept your bow because I need it to hunt the buffalo."

I watched. Grandfather seemed to be enjoying himself, playing with words, continuing to teach Mato Ska the ways of the Lakota.

He said, "We hunt the buffalo tomorrow, Mato Ska, but I think you are not yet ready. You must first practice with this bow—and with your new horse. Tomorrow you will watch the other hunters, to see how it is done. When you have practiced enough, then you will have your hunt." He looked at me. "Tomorrow you will watch Little Chief shoot a buffalo."

We left his tipi and walked to the river. I felt proud that Grandfather had included me with the other, more experienced hunters. Already I imagined demonstrating to

Mato Ska how to bring down a buffalo. I could see it in my mind—the galloping race, coming up behind the giant animal, the moment of victory when the arrow pierced the hide in just the right way. I was excited about the next day's hunt. Mato Ska interrupted my dreaminess.

"I can't stop thinking about my brother, Little Chief, wondering how he is, wondering if he is still looking for me, or if he has already left to become a doctor. My father wanted us both to be doctors—that is why he was so disappointed in me. He saved money to send us to school."

I heard the deep sadness in his voice. "But you are becoming a doctor, a medicine man. You helped Grandfather heal from his cough and fever."

Mato Ska seemed to straighten and grow taller. "You are right, Little Chief. I am studying to be a doctor. How could I have not realized that until you said it? Lakota medicine." He turned to look at me. "You have taught me so much, Brother. And I am grateful for my horse, and for Grandfather's bow, but it is the learning I get from the grandmothers that takes my heart."

"I know this, Mato Ska. I will call you Dr. White Bear."

Mato Ska laughed so hard the women at their cooking fires raised their heads to see what was so funny. "I think I am not yet ready for such a name, Little Chief—sir." He laughed again and said, "Yes, I will call you Sir Little Chief."

"*Hiya*! Grandfather would not like that. We better get to sleep. Tomorrow we hunt."

Mato Ska offered me his hand in the Lakota way of brothers. "I am happy here, Little Chief, more happy than I ever imagined I could be. I never want to go back, but know I must. There is too much still undone. I can't just run from it, or disappear, especially not from my brother."

"I know this. Grandfather says twins are connected for life, having been born from the same womb."

"I miss him," Mato Ska said.

"Soon. Soon we will go and see how he is."

20 A Foolish Hunter

When the birds first began their morning songs, I was up and ready. My body shivered with excitement at the possibility of shooting my second buffalo—and having Mato Ska witness it. I went to Unci's tipi and awakened him. He came out walking like an old man.

"What is the matter with you?" I asked him.

"I am stiff and sore from riding yesterday. My horse's backside and my bottom do not yet know each other well enough I am afraid."

"That is a problem, since today means much riding again."

Mato Ska groaned. "I have to go, Little Chief. My bottom will just have to put up with it."

When we met Grandfather, I explained the situation and he laughed. "It will get better as the day unfolds. I'll send the hunters out ahead and we'll follow more slowly. Sitting Bull says the herd is not far away today. I'll tell the others to ride out."

He left to talk to Crazy Horse and Mato Ska asked me, "Who is Sitting Bull?"

I told him the story of how Sitting Bull learned the movements of the buffalo and the other animals on the land by sitting and listening, and about the great bull buffalo killed by Crazy Horse. "His name comes from that sitting bull."

When Grandfather returned, we walked our horses out of the village. The hunters rode out ahead. Rabbit was with us. He was to hunt with us—to have another chance at killing his own buffalo. While we rode, Rabbit gave Mato Ska pointers about how to sit his horse so he could stay balanced and relaxed without straining. I was pleased to see my cousin and my white brother getting on so well.

Grandfather helped pass the hours by telling stories of the buffalo. He said the great beast was *Wakan Tanka's* gift to the Lakota people, the buffalo nation. The people honored that gift by using every part of the animal, from the tongue to the hide to the marrow of the bones.

Fascinated by the stories, and by the fact that nothing is wasted or taken for granted, Mato Ska asked many questions. Grandfather and Rabbit answered each one.

Mato Ska told more stories of his people. "Our god is a different god, Grandfather. My father says we must serve god on our knees, that god is the true authority and we are sinners."

Grandfather was intrigued. "So this god is a 'Sir'?"

He laughed. "I never thought about it, but yes, he is kind of a Sir God. We are his children—but I don't think the buffalo would be considered one of his children."

We spent a long time talking about the differences— and the sameness—between Sir God and *Wakan Tanka*. I listened with half an ear to their animated conversation. Mato Ska struggled to translate words from his language into Lakota. Often, it was not possible.

I realized that Grandfather desperately wanted to understand, and was actually learning from Mato Ska. This shocked me, that my White Bear would have something to teach our Lakota Elder. Of course Grandfather was trying to understand his own dream, the *maza* and the spider's web, and what it meant.

It dawned on me that I'd been so focused on teaching Mato Ska our ways that I'd made no effort to understand those who were coming—his people. I determined to make an effort to learn his language, just as Mato Ska had learned my language.

But not today. Today I would shoot my second buffalo, though I was not quite thirteen winters.

I kept the riders far ahead in view, wishing I had been allowed to ride with them instead of crawling like a turtle toward the hunting grounds. The day was fine, however, and I was excited when Grandfather finally said, "No more talk. Now we ride." We mounted the horses and rode the final stretch to catch up with the hunters.

When we reached them, the men laughed and teased, saying we should have stayed with the women this day. Mato Ska and Grandfather laughed, but I felt a twinge of embarrassment.

One of the scouts told us the buffalo were just over the ridge. From then on, we would use only sign language so as not to startle the herd. We rode up the ridge, got off our horses, and walked the final twenty paces. When Mato Ska saw the herd for the first time, he exclaimed loudly, only to take the angry stares of the men. This hushed him and he used only sign language from that point on. Grandfather pointed for Rabbit and me to go with the hunters. We followed them.

My heart thumped loudly and the blood hummed in my body. I wanted to ride fast and sure, to take down my second buffalo, to show Mato Ska how it is done. The hunters split into two groups. One group chased the herd our way and the buffalo began to run.

I was with the group riding the back edge of the herd and, as if on cue, we all began galloping up behind the animals. I quickly chose a young male and rode until I was coming up behind its right side. I stroked Wasaka's neck, talking to him, forming the important connection to my horse. As if hearing my thoughts and responding to them, Wasaka bounded forward in a fast gallop,

All was well. I had nearly come abreast of the buffalo and was preparing my arrow when, in a moment of stupidity, I glanced up to the ridge to see if Grandfather and Mato Ska were watching. In that split second, my concentration and connection with my horse broke. Wasaka shied to the right in a quick, jerky movement. I flew off his back and hit the ground hard. I blanked out a moment but somehow forced myself back into consciousness. I hardly knew what had happened, but my brain instantly registered the danger. The herd was on the run. In a few moments I would be trampled. My horse was gone; there was no time to signal him back.

Rabbit appeared, racing into the center of the danger. Just in time I saw his hand reaching out for me. I leapt to my feet, took Rabbit's hand, and he pulled me up behind him. We rode out of the stampeding herd and to safety before the pain even hit. I was panting, sweaty, covered with dust, and my right arm was skewed and crooked. I'd broken it.

Suddenly, the pain was excruciating; but the pain in my heart was even worse. It had happened fast but I knew, even in my pain-blurred fog, what I had done. I'd tried to show off for Mato Ska and ended up risking the life of my horse, myself—and Rabbit. When Grandfather walked over to me, I hung my head.

Mato Ska ran up and asked, "What happened? My god, you could have been killed."

Grandfather answered the question. "Little Chief didn't ride with his horse. His mind went elsewhere—and so his horse went elsewhere."

"I am ashamed, Grandfather."

He said, "You should be, Little Chief."

"Is Wasaka safe?"

Grandfather nodded. "Rabbit has gone after him." Then he called to several of the men and said, "Lay him down. We need to tend that arm."

One of the hunters took a thick piece of braided elk hide and told me to bite down on it. "This is going to hurt," he said.

Two of them held me steady while my uncle pulled the arm straight again. Pain, like lightning, flashed through my body and I cried out, but once the arm was straightened, it actually felt better. Mato Ska came forward a little shyly and said, "Let me bind it. I have done this before."

He took two of the arrows Grandfather had given him the night before and placed one arrow on either side of my arm. He then took lengths of rawhide and wrapped it, binding it firmly between the arrows, but not tight enough to cut the circulation.

"I was foolish, Mato Ska," I said. "I wanted so badly to show you how to kill the buffalo, I nearly killed myself and my horse."

Grandfather nodded. "A lesson you now know, Little Chief. And perhaps the right lesson for Mato Ska to have seen. A good hunter keeps his mind on his horse. We hardly ever have broken bones when we hunt." Then he softened his tone and knelt beside me. "Are you all right?"

Our hunting party returned to the village with the six buffalo Grandfather had said we needed. When my parents heard what had happened, shame rose up in my throat and I wanted to vomit. This was one story I did not want told.

By evening, the pain had worsened. I was freezing cold, and weak with dizziness. By nightfall, a fever had set in and I was barely aware when Unci came and took me to her tipi. There, she and Mato Ska tended me.

Unci instructed Mato Ska on how to cut thin willow branches and build a frame over me. I drifted in and out of fever dreams. Sometimes I was chasing that buffalo again, my skin melting into the hide of my horse, sometimes I was flying off the horse, but instead of hitting the ground I was like a cloud taking to the sky. Between these fever dreams, I saw Mato Ska place what looked like a miniature sweat lodge over my shivering body. I heard Unci's soft voice telling him how to cover the frame with skins, adding hot rocks from the fire under the covering. I felt a blast of warm steam hit my frigid body. I thought I was in the sweat lodge and tried to sing but my voice came out as a croak that made Unci laugh. When my body was covered with sweat, the lodge came off and Unci and Mato Ska bathed my body with cold water. The water smelled of sage tea and some medicine smell I couldn't recognize. I remember Unci's soft voice instructing Mato Ska about opening the pores of my skin to let the bad things out, and then washing them away with cool water.

Twice that night the process was repeated. I felt like I was steam and smoke rising from the floor of the tipi and moving out the hole, and into the heavens. I wondered what it would be like to die. Unci pried my mouth open and stuck a root under my tongue. She told me to keep it there, and the dreamy visions intensified. Toward early morning I heard birds, and the voice of my Grandfather beside me singing, his voice soft and low, calling me back from cloud, and smoke, and steam; calling me back to life.

When the sun rose fully, the fever was gone and I felt myself again, except for the throbbing pain in my arm and head. When I opened my eyes, Mato Ska slept beside me on the buffalo robe, his mouth slack and open. He looked like a small boy. His skin, now tanned and brown, no longer looked so white to me. "Brother," I whispered.

He opened his eyes and smiled. "You are better?"

"I am better. Thanks to Sir Doctor."

"Good. I was worried about you."

For the next several days I was confined to Unci's tipi. She and Mato Ska fed me herbal teas and thin broth made from buffalo bones to capture the healing marrow. I ate only small portions of meat and a rich berry soup, a *wojapi* that tasted sweet and wild on my tongue. Mato Ska spent many hours with me. We played our flutes and talked. I remembered my resolve to learn his language and began quizzing him in Lakota on how to say words in English. It passed the time. I did not have his ear for language and struggled with the unfamiliar sounds and rhythms.

When I was stronger, we walked along the creek, stepping in and out of the water. Within a week we shed our shirts and swam. Unci said the water would help heal my arm with its gentle massage. The cold water felt good. My arm was still bound, but after the second week they removed the arrows and bindings, and I was using it to swim.

Later that summer, my arm had nearly healed, although it ached on rainy days. I was still going to the creek daily to swim, to continue regaining my strength. During one of these outings, Mato Ska sat down beside the creek and asked, "How did you know what to play? The day you used the flute to let me know you were near?"

"I had watched you. I knew you got into trouble on purpose."

He looked up, surprised. "You knew?"

"Yes. I knew. The day your father beat you, I was watching. You could easily have made it to the little house. You didn't. I figured it must have been because you wanted to sit beside the creek with the birds and flowing water—so I played like birds and flowing water to reach you."

To my surprise, Mato Ska shifted the subject with a question. He asked, "And what would you play if you wanted a girl to notice you, if you wanted to reach a girl?"

"A girl?"

He grinned. "Yes, a girl. This girl keeps staring at me and I stare at her, but we never say anything."

"What girl?" I asked.

"I'll show you later."

He blushed and I laughed at my little brother who had been smitten by a girl.

"What is funny?"

"Nothing. I guess we are growing up. It pleases me that you are in love with a girl."

"I am *not* in love."

I was enjoying myself, not that I'd had much experience with girls either. I said, "Okay, so when you are *not in love* with a girl, here is what you do. You make a song and play it. If she likes your music, she will smile at you. If she doesn't smile, you have to give it up then, or try again later."

"That's it? Just play a song for her?" He picked up his flute and tried several different songs. "How do I know which song to play?"

"I don't know. Ask *Wakan Tanka*."

"Let me play one for you."

I shook my head and laughed. "It is not me you are playing for. What? You want me to smile at you?" I made girly faces at Mato Ska until we were both laughing.

While we were clowning around, a pretty girl walked to the creek not far from where we sat. Mato Ska went instantly quiet and I knew it was this girl who had caught his attention. Her name was Little Fawn, my cousin.

With shock, I realized in all of my time with Mato Ska, and the dream, and traveling to rescue him, I'd never once envisioned him with a Lakota wife and children, as a permanent part of our village. This confused me and I had the urge to talk to Grandfather about this.

Would the Elders agree that Mato Ska could marry a Lakota girl? Or was there more to my dream than I'd clearly seen, and Mato Ska would not remain with us but return to his people? Suddenly the bright day, the throb in my arm, my brother blushing on a rock, all receded in my confusion about Mato Ska's place among our people.

He pulled me back into the moment by asking, "Will you come with me? I think I know what song I should play."

Again I laughed. "No, I won't come with you. Have some courage, Little Brother. It is not me who likes her." I got up, slapped Mato Ska on the shoulder with my good hand, and left.

When I got back into the village, I went to Grandfather's tipi but he said Unci was looking for me, so I went to her instead.

She wanted to examine my arm to see how it was healing. She clucked and nodded as she rubbed a soothing ointment on it. I decided to ask Unci about the girl thing. "Mato Ska likes a girl, Grandmother."

She stopped rubbing, and paused for a long moment. "He will go back to his people some day?"

"I think he will, Grandmother."

"He must understand that it is unlikely that any of our girls would return with him, to live in his world. Unlikely. He would have to stay here if he took a Lakota wife. You should tell him this, Little Chief."

"Grandmother, I can't tell him. You must explain it to him. Or Grandfather. It is the place of the Elders to talk of such things."

She finished rubbing my arm and then took soft strips of hide and wrapped it tightly. "Your arm is healing well, but you must keep it firm for a while yet. The swimming is good for it. Send Mato Ska to me, Little Chief. I will talk of this with him."

When I came out of Unci's tipi, Mato Ska was walking back into the village. "Well?" I asked him.

He shook his head. "I lack courage. I picked up my flute and, suddenly, not a single song came to my mind. I failed."

"You are a puppy yet, Mato Ska," I teased him. "There is time. Unci wants to talk to you. Go to her."

Early the next morning, I went in search of Mato Ska pretending to want to do some practice with the bows but, in truth, I wanted to find out what Unci had said to him. It took no effort on my part to get him to talk. My brother was full of words this morning, but they were not the words I expected.

"I hardly slept at all last night," he began. "There is something I need to do."

I waited to hear more about Little Fawn, but Mato Ska did not have girls on his mind.

"Little Chief, I have to go and see my family. I've already talked to Grandfather and Unci and they agree that I should go. I want to stay here—this is my life now. Your people feel like my people, and I can hardly imagine living in that wooden cabin anymore but—your people are *not* my people. I can't stop thinking about my brother, or my mother, even my father. Last night, I woke up thinking something was happening with my brother. I need to go, Little Chief."

I wondered if this desire to go had come out of the talk with Unci, but I didn't ask. "I will go with you," was all I said.

Mato Ska nodded. "Grandfather said we should go early tomorrow. He told me again that twins have a special connection which begins in the spirit world, and that I can't undo that. It simply is." He looked at my arm. "Is your arm healed enough to travel?"

I nodded, "I have my own medicine man with me."

He shook his head. "I am far from being a medicine man. I couldn't even play my flute for a pretty girl."

21 The Third Journey South

Early the next morning, we loaded our horses with supplies and left the village. I was struck by the many changes that had taken place in the past year. We were older now, in our thirteenth year. This journey was like a reverse of the time I had traveled north with the white bear. Mato Ska was now a strong rider with his own horse. The clumsy gait was nearly gone; he sat his horse like a Lakota boy. And instead of spending the time teaching him the Lakota language, we now used the many hours on horseback to teach me the English words for tree, and sky, and stone.

Mato Ska told me of his world, a world of many people coming from over the oceans, of books and reading and schools, of trains and cities, of Sir God and sin. My mind was lit with the effort to make so many unfamiliar images.

Mato Ska had been born on the prairie but once, when he was eight, his family made a trip to visit relatives in a place he called St. Louis. He remembered being fascinated with the wide busy streets, the buildings lining the avenues, the people coming and going, the horses and wagons filled with goods.

"Who are all these people?" I asked. "Where do they come from?" I was trying to understand Grandfather's prophecy, of *maza* and spider webs and thunder sticks.

He said, "They come from many other nations, far away across the ocean. An ocean is big, like the prairie, only all water."

This image, more than any other, fired my mind. A prairie of water, a river so wide you could not see from bank to bank. I barely caught his next words.

"They come for many reasons." He seemed to consider this carefully before speaking. "I don't know all the reasons. Many were chased away. Many were starved off their lands. Others wanted the freedom to practice their own religions, to follow their own ways without persecution."

"Ah," I said, somehow relieved by this revelation. "Then these people would not be keen or strong about taking those things from others." I was thinking of the Lakota people, our lands and ways.

"I don't know, Little Chief. I think of Father. My father sees the world one way and believes that is the only way. I don't know what to say about that."

We rode on in silence for a long time, each caught in the trappings of our own memories and thoughts.

That night, camped beside a gentle stream, I dreamed again of bears. I had not had a bear dream since rescuing Mato Ska, but in this dream there were herds of black bears much like the herds of buffalo. They were crossing a giant land, lumbering and moving, and the black bears wore *maza*, metal collars, and growled in pain. In the dream, I stood on a high ridge watching this great gathering and migration of bears across the open land, and I knew I could not rescue them all. Could not. Somehow, the sight of it made my heart hurt. I felt all their pains and bleeding sores. In the dream, I had no choice but to turn and walk back down the ridge so I would not have to look at them. There were tears on my cheeks when I awoke.

The next morning, I said nothing about the dream. A dream such as that had to be absorbed slowly, its meaning tasted on my tongue for a long while until I could take it to Grandfather and ask him what it meant.

By late on the second day of our journey, we reached the steaming creek and knew we were close. Now that the moment had arrived, neither of us was sure about what would happen. I said, "We will go first and just observe— see what is going on at your home. But we should use sign language, and I don't want them to see me. You will have to approach them alone." I thought of the man's thunder stick and the metal ball in my pouch that had killed Grandfather's brother.

We reached the place along the creek where Mato Ska had once been tied to a tree. The cabin was just up the slope. I motioned for him to cross the creek. He did, pausing at the base of the tree and doing something on the bank I couldn't see. He turned and quickly came back across the creek into the underbrush where I hid. He held up a piece of paper and said, "My brother has left me a note. And there is food there. Mother must be bringing food to the creek for me." His voice caught in his throat.

"What does it say?"

He read aloud. "Dear Jonathan, Nobody knows what happened to you, but I feel in my heart that you are alive and safe. Father thinks you ran away because you don't like to work. He is still very angry. Mother cries and cries for you until he gets angry and then she goes quiet like a mouse. It is hard here without you, Jonathan. Thankfully, I am leaving to go east to become a doctor. If you should return, please, please let Mother know you are all right. I hope that when I return, I will be able to find you again. Love, James."

When he finished reading, his face was a storm of emotion. I felt his pain at finding out that his brother was gone, and that his mother was so sad. Out of respect, I waited until he had calmed himself before asking, "What do you want to do, Brother? It is your choice. I can't decide this for you."

"I know. Let me think."

Mato Ska walked alone up to the small, shallow cave where we had taken shelter during the storm. I stayed below, near the creek, watching the cabin for any signs of life. The mother and father were alone now, in the cabin, their sons both gone—off to be doctors I thought with a kind of smug satisfaction. I still felt the weight of the blows that man had given Mato Ska.

When he came back down from the ridge, he looked relieved, softer somehow, as if he had resolved something of great weight on his heart.

"I have decided what to do," he said.

"Tell me."

"I am returning with you to the village. My brother is gone. There is no reason for me to stay except to ease my mother's heart, and I have thought of a way to do that."

He explained that when he was a young boy, he had collected pretty stones and brought them to his mother as gifts. "In the cabin up there," he explained, "I am sure the window sills are still lined with my stones. I will leave a few stones beside the plate of food she leaves. In this way she will know I am alive, well, and thinking of her. It will not be the same as having me back, but it will ease her mind. Besides, she knows life would be difficult if I came back now."

With this decision made, he gently walked the banks of the river selecting stones for his mother's message. When his hands were full, he crossed the river and arranged the stones in a circle around the plate. "I want to wait until the evening meal time—to see if she brings a new plate, to know if she has seen the stones. I need to at least see her," he whispered, his voice breaking.

We spent the rest of the late afternoon up in the small cave opening. The branches were still there, leafless now, and the late sunlight reached our heads and warmed them.

When the supper hour had passed, we heard someone approaching. I signed to him to be silent and together we crept to a place where we were completely hidden but could watch the creek.

His mother came down the slight slope, a plate in her hand, her head bowed and covered with a bonnet. I watched as Mato Ska's fingers unconsciously reached for her through the screen of branches, as if sending her his thoughts the way I send my thoughts to Wasaka.

We could not hear well, but when she reached the plate with the stones arranged prettily around it, we saw her pull back and open her mouth in a gasp. She fell to her knees on the ground and wept, picking up each stone one by one and turning it. She took one smooth stone and put it on her tongue as if tasting it, tasting her son. Mato Ska wept silently as he watched, but he was smiling. When she had touched each stone and tucked them into her deep skirt pockets, she stood up. Her face was lit with a beautiful smile, her eyes bright with tears, and before she turned to go back up to the cabin, she searched all the surrounding trees and hillsides for her son.

We held our breath. Finally, the woman waved, smiled again, and turned toward the cabin. She apparently accepted that, for whatever reason, her lost son had returned—but would not stay.

I looked at Mato Ska and then silently pointed downstream. Together, we left the place by the river where a young boy had once been tied to a tree. I thought the man beside me bore little resemblance to that boy, that white bear I had released. His face was wet with tears, but his step was firm.

It was not yet dark so we rode silently and quickly, as if the wind rushing around us, or the feel of horse flesh between our thighs would dissolve any conflict, any pain or grief, maybe even the memory of what we had left behind.

When the trail was too dark to see, we stopped, took the robes off the horses and made camp. We ate a few bites of the food my mother had packed and went immediately to sleep.

Before the birds had even begun singing, Mato Ska tapped me on the shoulder and we again rolled the buffalo robes, climbed on our horses, and rode off into the day.

Wasaka and Eyakpakpa seemed to sense our urgency to get back to the village. We rode hard all day, scarcely talking, scarcely stopping until, by late evening, we were again riding toward the village. Only then did we slow the horses to a trot. Mato Ska looked at me and said, "My brother has gone away to become a doctor."

"Yes, and you have gone away to become a doctor, just as your father wanted."

He smiled, but the smile did not quite reach his eyes. "Yes, just as my father wanted."

22 Seasons Passing

Mato Ska stayed with us for four years. The seasons passed from winter to spring to summer, and back toward winter as we, both in our own ways, settled into manhood. During the third summer since Mato Ska had chosen to stay, I met a pretty girl from another clan. We found each other beneath a giant cottonwood tree when the insects were humming so loud we could hardly speak. We needed few words as it turned out, so instantly did our spirits link up. I took her as my wife the day before her family left to travel west to their winter grounds. Her name was Morning Dove.

Mato Ska took no wife. I often wondered what Unci had said to him after his infatuation with Little Fawn. When I finally asked, he laughed, remembering his struggle to find a pretty song for a pretty girl. He told me, "Unci explained that marrying a Lakota girl meant promising to stay forever here—to never return to my brother. I could not make such a promise."

His answer was plainspoken, without heat, without pain. I understood and we never spoke of it again. Mato Ska learned to hunt. He and Rabbit killed their first buffalo on the same day and this, more than anything, strengthened the bond between them although, after his first kill, he declined hunting in favor of his studies.

Little Fawn married Rabbit. She and Morning Dove became great friends and adopted Mato Ska as a brother. They fussed over him constantly, teasing and feeding him, and perhaps taking away any sadness he had at having no wife to call his own.

When Little Fawn bore a first son to Rabbit, Mato Ska did not attend the birth. Unci would not allow him to tend the women in childbirth, so he sat outside Rabbit's tipi and played his flute, using his music to lure the infant out of the womb and into the world, just as I had wooed him with my music.

Rabbit named his son *Mato*, Bear. This naming somehow completed our circle. I had killed my first buffalo before Rabbit. And he had become a father before I did, and Mato Ska and I had a new nephew named for the dream that had pulled us together. Our circle was complete.

Life in our camp was peaceful during those years.

Mato Ska said he could not be a proper student without paper and pencil, and so he taught himself to make paper from plant and wood fibers that he cooked and then pressed between slabs of wood until the water was removed. What remained was a clear, greenish paper. On this he drew small pictures of plants, wrote his thoughts and what he was learning, and named things. He kept the pages in a leather bundle he created just for this purpose. The children, fascinated with his scribbling, asked to be taught, so he taught them the English alphabet.

He even learned to write Lakota words by ear so the alphabet could be used to learn simple words and sentences. In time, he had created a little school in the camp and the children spent hours with his paper, scraps of bark or hide, and a piece of charcoal learning to make the letters. Mato Ska, however, was more interested in learning about the Lakotas than he was about teaching the children about the world he knew—and had left behind.

I watched my brother grow in this way. Gone was the boy I had rescued—he'd been replaced by a quiet, gentle man who liked the children and the grandmothers.

Ever since the day he had talked with Unci about Little Fawn, he had not approached a girl with a song but seemed content to have Little Fawn and Morning Dove as sisters. Instead of being a husband or father, he channeled all of his energy toward learning the healing arts from Unci, and teaching the children. The people began to depend upon him almost as much as they depended on the grandmothers. The children, especially, liked to have Mato Ska treat their small wounds, the bloody scratches from branches or punctures from raspberry thorns, and the fevers that painted their cheeks bright red.

Nobody in the village ever thought about Mato Ska being a white man anymore. Occasionally the hunters and scouts reported seeing a party of white people traveling across the land, usually far to the south where Mato Ska's family lived, and the reports increased as the years went by. We again traveled further north to avoid contact, continuing to live life as we had, with the days curling into night and the seasons passing as we followed the buffalo. I was a man now and worked hard to bring meat to our people, to care for my wife, and to tend to what needed tending.

Mato Ska moved into his own tipi about the time I married Morning Dove. He set it up between Unci's tipi and ours. He ate most meals with us and we spent many evenings singing, playing the flute, telling stories, and teaching Morning Dove some English words. She had a sharp mind, my little wife, and we were often amazed at the skillful way she used both Lakota and English, making jokes and word play—getting us laughing so hard we had to press our hands to our bellies.

One night Mato Ska said, "I wish you had a twin, Morning Dove. I would marry her in a moment."

His voice sounded wistful and lonely. He was a man caught between worlds, with no wife or family. The reference to twins made me think again of his brother. Little had been said about his brother or family since the day we left the stones beside the plate, but I knew he had not forgotten. I often saw a shadow of sadness cross his face like a cloud on a sunny day, but I left it to him to consider.

In this way four winters passed. By the summer I reached my seventeenth year, Morning Dove was expecting our first baby. Her belly was round and hard and Unci said the baby would come before the cool breezes of fall. The scorching summer heat was hard on her. She tired easily and sometimes, feeling faint, she would go to the river and plant her body in the middle of the water to let the cool waters flow around her until her mind cleared again.

"You look like a young beaver floating out there, only your nose poking above the surface," I teased, but I also worried. I'd seen many women not survive the birth bed, and I stayed close to the village to help her with her daily work. Mato Ska often brought her tonics and teas to keep her blood flowing, and to keep the water from gathering in her ankles and calves.

I had become so accustomed to the working rhythm of our lives that it startled me to be awakened early one morning by Mato Ska urgently calling my name outside our tipi. I rose and went out. "What is it, Brother?"

"Something is happening with my brother, Little Chief. I dreamed of him all night long. I think he calls my name. I have to go see what is wrong."

Mato Ska was clearly upset, and my first thought was for Morning Dove, but I realized she was still weeks from delivering and the grandmothers would take good care of her. "I'll go with you." I said.

He smiled. "I figured you would. Can we go now?"

"I need to go and talk to Grandfather first. You get the horses ready."

I went to Grandfather's tipi and told him. "We'll ride, quickly, Grandfather," I said, "We will return within five days."

Since our last trip to the steaming river, Grandfather had grown more toward the spirit world. I saw it in his eyes. He seemed to look beyond me to some other place, and he often remained in his tipi for entire days, resting and gathering his strength for the next long journey he would make. I was shocked to see tears in the old man's eyes on this early morning. "Grandfather, what is it?"

"Nothing. I was dreaming of my brother. We were not twins but we, too, were deeply connected."

I fingered the pouch at my neck that still contained the heavy, metal ball. "The brother who died from this?" I asked.

"Yes, that one. Before you go, there is something you must do, Little Chief. You will soon be a father, but you are not yet fully a man. It is time for you to get your feather, time for you to fast, and go out to do this. Mato Ska will go with you to support you and to learn, but only you will seek a feather."

"But Grandfather, Mato Ska wants to . . . ."

"No, Little Chief. It must be now."

I had been waiting for this day, for Grandfather to give me this task. That it would come now, when Mato Ska was so anxious to find his brother, somehow filled me with foreboding. I looked at my Grandfather carefully but could read no more from the lines of his face, the curve of his brow. He was firm. I must first get my feather.

Grandfather said, "Tell Mato Ska he must do this. When you bring back your feather, we will celebrate both of you with a feast and dancing, and then you can go to his family." He grew quiet again and I watched him. He asked, "Will Mato Ska return?"

"I don't know, Grandfather. Only he can make that decision. We don't yet know what calls him to return."

"I will pray for you, Grandson, for both of you. I will ask *Wakan Tanka* to keep you safe. But first, get your feather."

"Thank you, Grandfather."

I left, distress low down in my belly, but it was not about getting my feather, or Mato Ska's journey; it was about Grandfather. The old man would not long be with us. I felt this in my bones. I could not imagine the village without Grandfather. Distracted, I went first to my tipi where Morning Dove still slept. I kissed her and told her I was to go out on the hill and get my feather.

She nodded sleepily and smiled. "Go, I will be fine here."

Mato Ska was loading a pack of food onto the back of his horse when I walked up. "You can leave that pack behind, my brother."

"Leave the food? What are you thinking?"

"A change of plans. Grandfather has told me to go first and get my feather. We can leave after I have done this. You are to come as my helper. It will only mean a day's delay."

I saw conflict skitter across Mato Ska's face, and said, "I know you want to ride to your brother, but Grandfather does not ask these things without a purpose. I must do it. You are to be with me to learn, so you will know what to do when you take your feather. It is an honor. It is the next move toward manhood."

I knew the moment Mato Ska accepted the change in our plans. He nodded and asked, "Can we eat before we go?"

"Ahh," I laughed. "A hungry man is a healthy man. Yes, first we eat and drink our fill, but then there will be no food or water until we return. Grandfather intends a fast— and then a feast to honor us both when it is done."

Mato Ska unpacked the leather bag of food and we went and ate and drank at his tipi. It was still early and I did not want to disturb Morning Dove from her sleep again.

Grandfather and Morning Dove would tell my parents where I'd gone. I knew Father would be proud, Mother too.

When we finished, we cleared the scraps away, took a final long drink of water, and went out into the dim morning. The sky was overcast and clouds hung heavy above the village. Before we left, I stopped before Sitting Bull's tipi. He was seated outside in the gray light. I told Mato Ska to wait a minute and I went and asked Sitting Bull where I should go to get my feather.

He said, "So, you want to know where my *kola* are flying?" He picked up a stick and drew a quick map, indicating a rocky canyon less than half a day west of the village. "Here, Little Chief. You will find my friends here, a family of golden eagles." He looked up at Mato Ska sitting on his horse and said, "You are going to see a beautiful thing, my friend. Watch and he will show you how it is done."

"Thank you, Cousin." I said, and then we mounted our horses and rode out of the village.

23 Taking a Feather

As if a sign from *Wakan Tanka,* the clouds cleared as the sun rose slowly over the eastern horizon and the day dawned with the sky a clear, vivid blue. Excitement simmered in my body. Soon, I would be a full man of my people. "Taking a feather is a beautiful thing, Mato Ska. You have not seen this before. I hope it goes well and the eagle will let me take a feather."

"What do you mean? How can an eagle let you *take* a feather?"

I smiled. "You will see, my brother. I will not get a feather unless the eagle allows it." I explained that we were going two hours west to a rocky cliff where the eagles nested. All this day I would not eat or drink. We would prepare a blind along the cliff where I would spend the night.

Just as Sitting Bull had indicated, we reached a rocky ridge opening into a larger canyon. There was a small falls, the water tumbling into a creek at the bottom, and there we made camp. "This is a good place, Mato Ska. You will be able to see. Look, there is the nest."

High up on a rocky ledge we could just make out two beautiful golden eagles perched in the nest. The cliff was high, and it made the sun appear to be going down even though there were many hours of daylight left.

"There," I said, "that is where my feather will come from if *Wakan Tanka* is with me." It was as if the eagles heard my words. The pair spread their wings and lifted off the cliff effortlessly, meeting the wind as natural as a fish swims. They glided, sometimes appearing to stop midair, sometimes streaming up or down.

I felt the power of this place where eagles hunt and mate, where hard stone and soft earth collide. It filled my chest with eagerness again. "Come. I have to prepare. You will go hunting and shoot me two rabbits, Mato Ska."

"But you said we were to have no food."

"It is not food for us. Go, and you will see how it is done."

While Mato Ska hunted, I placed my buffalo robe on the ground in sight of the eagles and prayed to *Wakan Tanka* to guide me in taking a feather, to speak to the eagles for me, to explain that soon I would be a father and needed a man's full strength. I had been son and grandson; I had been boy and then young man; and now I would be a father and a man. The prayers formed in my mind as easily as music came from my flute. The wind touched my cheeks, lifted my hair, and I felt held aloft like the eagles. I sang the words aloud, letting the wind take them up to the pair of eagles who had returned again to their perch. It felt as if my ribs were cracking, my heart trying to leap from my chest, so large was this moment.

When Mato Ska returned he carried two rabbits. "I was successful."

"Good. Wrap them in a piece of leather and hang them high in the tree. We don't want any animals to carry them off while we are gone."

"Where are we going?" Mato Ska asked.

"Up there." I pointed to a shadow, a deep cut in the canyon wall at some distance from the eagles' nest, but about the same height.

The climb was difficult, but I noticed how strong and sure Mato Ska's feet were on the small ledges and dips of the canyon. The awkward boy I had rescued was awkward no longer. His hair was long and golden, flowing loose behind his ears. When we reached the ledge, I saw that the place was perfect. Before I prepared it, however, I said, "Let's go to the top first. I want to show you something."

With a final tugging effort, we reached the top of the canyon wall. I led him to a small stone outcropping that jutted out into the canyon. Below us the land flowed down and out to the prairie floor. "Look, Mato Ska."

"I'm looking. It is incredible."

"Now, go very near to the edge and close your eyes."

Mato Ska grinned. "How close?"

"Close. I promise not to push you off. Just do it."

We moved to the very edge of the outcropping. "Now close your eyes," I said, closing my own as well. A stream of air rose up from the canyon depths and reached my face, lifting the small hairs off my brow. "Keep your eyes closed, Mato Ska, and then raise your arms out from your sides like wings. Now open your eyes and see nothing above, nothing below, only the world as one. Then close your eyes again and drink it all in."

I raised my own arms experiencing the same lift and strength of the wind that carried the eagles through the sky. It was powerful, this sensation of flight, this scent of pine and earth, this feeling of leaving earth to soar the heavens.

Mato Ska whispered, as if hard sound would be too much for this moment, "I'm flying, Little Chief."

"I am too. We are eagle brothers. There are no problems that can touch us here." I dropped my arms and looked at him. His yellow hair was flying back, his arms lifted, his eyes still closed; I felt love and pride for my friend pierce my heart. The piercing was almost painful, like a knife. We stayed for a long time on the edge of the cliff, drinking in the wide, dangerous world below but remaining untouched by it. Finally I said, "Come. We have a lot of work to do and not much daylight left."

Following Grandfather's instructions, I directed Mato Ska to gather whatever branches and slim leafy sticks he could find. I helped. When we had a nice bundle we made our way down to the ledge to the cut into the canyon I'd found earlier. We took the branches and wove them into a screen, or blind, to cover the small, man-sized opening into the cliff. The space reminded me of the cave opening where Mato Ska and I had first come to know each other only this landing had eagle droppings, a good sign.

Creating the blind didn't take long. Finally, I climbed behind the branchy screen and said, "This is where I will spend the night. You will be down below watching out for me. Here, I will wait for my feather."

Mato Ska said, "If we looked, I think we could probably find a feather."

I shook my head. "No, that would not be the same. The eagle must *give* me a feather, and I must *take* a feather. It is a contract. We should pray now." We sat on the ledge and sent our songs and prayers out to *Wakan Tanka*. Again the breeze crawled up the canyon wall and touched my face, my knees, my feet.

With the prayer completed, we climbed back down to the main camp. Mato Ska went to the edge of the creek and dropped to his knees to take a drink. "No," I said, "You are not to drink either. You are my helper and must also fast."

He looked up. "I am thirsty from all that work."

I laughed "Yes, baby boy, but you are not to drink or eat until we get back. You take your thirst and your hunger and you offer it to *Wakan Tanka* as a sacrifice. You'll see. The more thirst and hunger you feel, the stronger your prayers will be. Pray through your thirst and hunger."

"What about the rabbits? If we can't eat them, what are they for?"

"You'll soon understand."

I went to the creek and cleansed myself without drinking. Mato Ska did the same. The water was inviting, almost alive. He chuckled, "That water looks pretty good to me right now."

"Pray, Mato Ska. Pray."

When it was nearly dark, we again climbed to the ledge and the blind we had prepared. We brought both rabbits. I went into the enclosure carrying one rabbit with me, and instructed Mato Ska to close me in with the remaining leafy branches.

"Now set the other rabbit on the ledge where I can still reach him with one hand. Then you can go back down. Build a small fire if you want, it won't matter. It will be a powerful thing. Stay awake if possible—to feel all this night will contain. The eagle will hunt when the light breaks. It will be worth watching."

Mato Ska said nothing more but disappeared over the edge and went back down to the camp. I listened to make sure he did not fall off—the darkness was getting more complete and I didn't want my brother to injure himself.

My arm throbbed from the exertion of climbing the cliff wall. The bone I had broken in my arm continued to remind me not to be foolish, never to show off my skills again. I thought back to that time and saw myself a boy, not a man. What changes time had brought. And now I sat behind a blind of branches on a stony floor waiting for eagles to fly and hunt.

My belly rumbled and my tongue felt dry and gritty. I did as I had told Mato Ska to do and prayed through hunger and thirst. All night long I prayed; sometimes singing my prayers, sometimes speaking them, sometimes just feeling them emanate from my exhaustion and my hunger. Every time the image of a person I loved—or a person I did not love—appeared, or every time a fleeting thought entered the field of darkness behind my eyes, I offered it all up to *Wakan Tanka*. As the night deepened, so did my prayers. Soon I felt myself a part of the rock on which I sat, a part of the branches that closed me in. The outline of my own body seemed to disappear and I felt as if I were floating around the earth like dust or smoke.

Never before had my prayers reached the root of my own spirit in this way. It was both exhilarating and exhausting. Occasionally, my head dipped and fell toward my chest but I jerked it upright again and continued praying. I thought of the babe in Morning Dove's womb, a babe that I would soon feed and teach, a son or daughter. I offered my child to *Wakan Tanka* for safety and protection.

It was the longest night of my life, and yet it seemed in an eye blink the sky turned a deep, deep blue, the blue of prayer and wintry skies. I forced myself to crawl back into my body and be alert once again. Soon the eagles would hunt. Soon I would know if they would offer me a feather.

I reached a hand out through the blind and took a foot of the rabbit that had been placed there. I held fast, knowing the eagle's hunt would be only seconds long. I prayed for the eagle to land, to take the rabbit, to allow me to take a feather. My hand cramped from holding the rabbit's foot and my tongue was thick in my mouth, but the deep blue was cracking as the first beams of the sun broke through.

Suddenly, it was as if the wind pierced the branch enclosure; a strong gust hit my face. It was fast, so fast. I heard a great fanning sound, of wings and wind, and I clutched the rabbit foot hard. Through the lace of branch and leaf I saw the male golden eagle land. I surged forward and took one of the eagle's feet. It felt like cracked leather beneath my fingers. At the same time I took the eagle's foot, I released the rabbit's foot. It was a split second dance between the eagle and me. With my free hand I grabbed a tail feather, held it hard, and then let go of the eagle's leg.

And it was done. The eagle was gone. The rabbit was gone. And the feather in my hand was the most precious thing I'd ever seen.

I drew it in through the branches and looked at it. It was long and fine, the color of tree bark, but oiled and sleek. The eagle had honored me by leaving a feather. I could barely breathe. I took the fine, pale piece of soft leather I'd brought with the hope of wrapping such a feather inside. I wrapped the feather and put it into the same pouch I carried my flute in, and the metal ball, and then I crawled out of the enclosure. My legs were stiff and cold from the long night of sitting in the cramped space, but my heart rejoiced.

Along the edge of the cliff where the eagles nested, I watched the male take the rabbit to his mate, to feed her first, and I thought of Morning Dove, my mate, the mother of my child. I took the second rabbit and laid it out on the ledge in thanks. This one was for the male eagle. I climbed down to where Mato Ska waited.

He gave a shout and raced to me, shaking my hand and then hugging me. "I saw it, Little Chief. I saw the eagle land. You did it, didn't you?"

I pulled the leather from my pouch. "He did it, Mato Ska. He gave me a feather."

An eagle screamed high up above their nest, as if confirming my words.

Our return ride to the village passed quickly. I was tired, hungry, and thirsty, but felt the change in my body, the widening of my spirit. I tried to find words to describe the experience, but there were no words. "You will soon get your feather, Mato Ska. And then you will have this experience and not just hear about it."

He was quiet for a long while and then said, "Little Chief, your family has taken me as a brother, as a grandson, but I can't stop thinking about my own family. It is not yet done with them. When the feast is over tonight, I need to leave."

I looked at him and smiled. "Maybe we can get one night's sleep?"

He closed the gap between us and clipped my shoulder. "Okay, maybe one night."

When we arrived, the feast was already being prepared. The hunters had gone out the day before and killed an elk. The village buzzed with the news that I had gotten my feather. Young children swarmed around Mato Ska like bees while he told the story of the eagle coming.

I went to Grandfather's tipi and showed him the eagle's gift.

"I knew you'd get that feather. It is good, Little Chief. Let me hold it for you. Tonight I will put it in your hair and we will celebrate."

All that evening I felt detached from the celebration, from the stories of other hunters and how they had gotten their feathers, from the children playing and the women talking. I felt distant and alone, but it was not a bad thing. Morning Dove sent me worried glances, but I just smiled at her, feeling weary to my bones.

When Grandfather placed the feather in my hair, I felt as if this was the end of something—and not the beginning. I wondered if Grandfather would give me a new name as he had with other young men, but he did not. Instead, he tied the feather and said, "Be *wasaka,* Little Chief. Always be strong."

I couldn't shake the feeling from the night before, of leaving my own skin behind and entering some new place. My spirit no longer felt contained within my body alone but was out there, like the eagles, roaming the skies.

Finally I went to Morning Dove and said, "Come. I want to rest and I want you and our child with me. Tomorrow I take Mato Ska to see his family again." I kissed her, then bent and kissed her rounded belly. The small action brought tears to my eyes. "I need you with me, Morning Dove."

I spoke briefly with Mato Ska about the next day's departure, and then I went with my wife to our tipi and stretched out on the soft buffalo robes. We lay, side by side, staring out to the stars above. I told her all that had happened the night before.

Morning Dove was quiet, listening. Finally she spoke. "I think the eagle has changed you, my husband. Something is different. I can't find you."

I rolled over and took her in my arms. "I am right here beside you."

"Yes, your body is beside me, but your spirit flew off to some other place. Will it come back, I wonder?"

She put into words what I had been feeling. Morning Dove sounded sad and I sought the words to comfort her, but nothing came. When I looked again she was fast asleep, her face soft and smooth. I kissed her forehead and finally allowed myself to drift into a deep, dreamless world of sleep.

24 The Fourth Journey South

Morning Dove brought us packs of food for our journey. I kissed her and rubbed a hand along her hard belly. "Take care of my son, little mother."

She grinned. "Or daughter?"

"A daughter would be fine with me—especially if she is beautiful like her mother."

She hugged me then and told me to go. She was still grinning, her hair blue-black and shining in the morning sun. I will never forget the vision of her face and that shining hair, not if I drift through time for a thousand years.

Mato Ska had both horses ready and was impatiently waiting on the edge of the village. I hung the pack of food on the back of his horse and we rode out quietly so as not to disturb the sleeping village. Finally we reached the open plain and broke into a fast gallop.

We spoke little and concentrated on the earth passing beneath our feet, riding until dark and then sleeping until the birds awoke and riding again. The trip was uneventful. We saw no one and reached the steaming river by late afternoon on the second day.

Mato Ska was agitated, his body restless, his eyes searching. We followed the river in toward the homestead. I knew he sought his brother, his twin. "What do you think we will find?" I asked.

"I don't know," he said. "My brother is in my mind. I have not felt him this way for a long while . . . since we came the last time. It could be he has just returned from the east and is seeking me again."

I didn't need to tell Mato Ska to use sign language. In the years he'd spent with us he had become Lakota. His instincts were good, his feet quiet, his eyes sharp. As we approached the place by the creek where he had been tied, we were completely silent. We watched the slope to the cabin for signs of life. There were horses in the corral, smoke curling from the chimney, all signs the homestead was still occupied.

We watched, unsure of what to do, and so we just waited. Finally, as the sun began to hang lower in the sky, Mato Ska tapped me on the shoulder and pointed. Two people, a man and a woman, not his parents, emerged from the cabin door and began walking down toward the creek. They were holding hands, laughing and talking, the man motioning to distant points along the horizon. Once, he leaned over and kissed the woman on the lips and she smiled at him, pointing back toward the cabin. She left him and returned to the cabin, while the man continued on down to the creek.

Mato Ska's breathing nearly stopped. As the man approached, I saw an almost exact duplicate of my brother, only this man was dressed in fine cloth, a dark coat and shining shoes, his hair short and slicked close to his head above his snowy white shirt. I jokingly signed to Mato Ska that this handsome, strong man looked nothing like my ugly brother.

He stabbed at my arm with a fist and mouthed the words, "Don't be a dog."

Clearly the twin brother was in fine health—and had taken a woman. I thought Mato Ska must be relieved that the call he'd felt was not a call of distress.

When the man reached the river, he sat down on the bank in the exact spot where Mato Ska had been tied repeatedly as a boy. This time there was no plate of food, no sign of what had happened in that place. A great loneliness showed in the man's face, in the curve of his shoulders, in the way he stared at the water flowing by. He picked up a small stone, tossed it into the creek, and watched the rings ripple out.

Seemingly without a thought, Mato Ska picked up a stone the same size as the one his brother had just tossed and flipped it into the river. The small plop it made as it hit the water was almost inaudible, but James raised his head and looked around. He picked up a larger stone and tossed it into the water. Mato Ska picked up a larger stone and tossed it.

A small smile crept across James's face. He tossed a third stone. Mato Ska tossed a third stone and then signed for me to remain hidden. He stepped out from behind a tree and stood on the opposite bank from his brother.

I watched, my heart thumping in my chest, as the two brothers saw one another for the first time in many years.

The well-dressed man said, "Jonathan?"

Mato Ska nodded and stepped into the creek and crossed over.

James dropped his hands to his sides, stared, and then cried out, "Jonathan. My god, it is you!" The two men flung their arms around each other. Mato Ska shushed his brother for fear of raising the parents from the cabin. James was crying now, and so was Mato Ska. It was as if the two brothers had been starved for the sight of each other, the feel of each other.

I now knew enough English to understand their words, and I knew Mato Ska well enough to understand the connection these two men shared in their hearts. I felt oddly alone, standing hidden in the bushes, my white brother now across the river in the embrace of his twin. We had been connected for so long, I had forgotten that this bond would be stronger. The brothers conversed in whispers, each with tears in their eyes, the urge to touch and hug one another not to be resisted.

My loneliness did not last long, however. Mato Ska called softly for me to come. I had no desire to encounter the father's thunder stick and scanned the area carefully, looking toward the cabin before stepping out and crossing the stream.

When James first saw me, there was a flash of alarm. Mato Ska said quietly, "James, this is my brother, Little Chief. He is the one who took me to his village." Mato Ska watched the two of us face each other.

James stepped forward, "Then he is my brother as well." He offered me a hand. I took it near the elbow and James, confused at first, quickly adjusted his own grasp to match mine. He turned again toward Mato Ska and said, "God's eyes but you look good. Look at your hair, your clothing. You look like an Indian."

Mato Ska laughed. "I am an Indian. I am Lakota now. They have taken me as one of their own."

James eyed me a second time, and then turned and said to Mato Ska, "We have much to talk about, you and I," he pointed toward me, "and your brother as well."

Before the conversation could progress, however, we heard a woman's voice calling for James. I was ready to scamper into hiding but James touched my arm and said, "That is Emily Traub, my fiancé. I will introduce both of you. Don't worry, she will say nothing."

Emily came over the small rise leading down to the riverbank and she stopped, her mouth rounding into a gasp, "Oh-h. James?" She looked from one brother to the other, and then at me. "Goodness, what is this?"

I saw no fear in her eyes, only a bright curiosity curving her pretty brows upward. This white woman was quite different from the very little I'd seen of Mato Ska's meek mother. Her hair was light brown, smoothly braided, the braids wound atop her head. A pretty collar touched her chin and hugged her neck and she wore a dress that covered her entire body, the skirt flowing to the ground and covering the tips of shiny black boots. I waited, saying nothing.

James went to her, held her arms, and said, "Emily, my brother has come back. Come, I want to introduce you."

He introduced her to Jonathan. She went immediately and gave him a hug. James introduced her to me and she politely put her arms up and gave me a girlish hug as well, smiling and saying, "I never dreamed I'd meet an Indian brother. Three brothers. And all so handsome."

I said, in not quite perfect English, "It is good to meet you."

"No, the pleasure is all mine, sir." she said, and then gave me a pretty bow.

"I am not a sir," I said, the words coming unbidden to my mouth.

Mato Ska laughed and explained to James and Emily our many conversations about the word 'sir.'

We sat on the grassy bank. James and Jonathan talked in quick, short sentences, each trying to tell the other all that had happened since the day Jonathan had disappeared. I caught only snatches of it and kept my eye on the path leading up to the cabin, watching for any sign of the parents coming.

There was talk about going east to the cities, becoming a doctor, meeting Emily Traub who was studying to be a nurse. There was talk about Unci and training in the healing arts, about hunting and the great generosity of the Lakota people. The words flew back and forth until I grew dizzy from trying to understand. I had never heard English spoken between two who shared the language. It was quite a different thing than my own halting conversations with Mato Ska.

Finally James went silent, looking at his brother. "Why did you leave, Jonathan? I sensed you were not dead—in fact I was sure you were alive, but why? It nearly broke our mother into two pieces when you disappeared. We searched and searched. I found the little cave up above, and horse tracks. We knew you were not alone, but we didn't know if you were safe, or had been taken captive by the savages."

Mato Ska scowled at his brother. "Have you heard nothing I've said? My Lakota people are not savages."

James recanted. "I'm sorry, Jonathan." He cast a glance at me. "I did not think before I spoke. Back east there is all manner of talk about the native savages. It slipped out of my mouth."

"You must not listen to such talk. For the past five years I have lived with Little Chief and his people. They are kind and generous, strong hunters, and they share everything they own with each other." He pointed at his own beautiful buckskin clothing. "They have given me everything—everything—even though I was not like them."

In that moment, I felt proud of my white bear. It was as I had dreamed, that I would teach this boy Lakota ways and he would tell others. I turned to James and, in halting, slow English, said, "Your brother has also become a doctor."

"What do you mean, Little Chief?"

"He says we have given him everything, but he has hunted, worked beside us, studied the healing medicines with Unci, and has given as much back as we have given to him."

James appeared to consider this carefully. "I want to hear everything, Jonathan. We have so much to talk about. And Mother and Father will be amazed to find you still alive—and looking so well."

I watched Mato Ska's face. It was like watching rough water; a mixture of desire and loathing, of conflict. Finally he said, "I don't want to stay, James. I cannot forget that tree, the way Father beat me because I was not strong like you."

James looked stunned. "You don't want to even see them?"

"I don't know. I don't know what I want. My life is good with Little Chief and his people. It feels like the right place for me. How can I make you understand?"

"But Father will send you east too. You can study to be a real doctor."

A stab of anger zinged through my body. "Your brother is a real doctor. He is nearly a medicine man in our village."

Mato Ska rested a hand on my shoulder. "This is between James and me, Little Chief. You don't need to defend me. I am strong enough now to do that for myself."

Instead of responding in anger, Mato Ska told his brother all about his life in the village, the way the people did not try to tame nature but lived within her gentle arms. He described the generosity, the peaceful ways of the village. He talked about the children and how they came to him for stories, and for help with their cuts and bruises. "It is my place, James. I fit there in ways I could never fit here—or out east."

James listened with great attention, nodding, sometimes taking Emily's hand and squeezing it tight. "I have wronged you, Jonathan, and your friend. I can see what they have done for you. My god you look so strong and sure of yourself. I think the ways out east would have crushed your spirit." He laughed. "They nearly crushed mine. I think I am a little jealous of this life you have led."

Mato Ska kicked at the dirt. "That would be a first— for you to be jealous of me. You can't imagine how I tried to be like you—until I finally gave up trying. I actually got into trouble on purpose so Father would bring me down here. Even tied to a tree was better than working so hard to be something I was not."

James looked troubled. He put his hand on his brother's shoulder and said, "I wanted to defend you. I tried. But it only seemed to make things worse for you. I'm sorry, Jonathan."

"You have nothing to be sorry for. It was not you—it was him."

The silence held for a long moment. The only sound came from water flowing down the river—taking the past with it. I was not sure what Mato Ska would do next. I waited for a sign from him.

James initiated the next move. He said, "Shall I tell them I saw you? Father is still, well, Father; angry, discontent, but he is good to Mother. He treats her well, but I'm not sure how he would treat you even now."

Again storms flew across the sky of Mato Ska's face, but finally he turned to James and said, "I know this. Say nothing, James. I will return with Little Chief. It is enough I got to see you, to let you know I am safe and doing well." He glanced at Emily. "And I can see now that you are doing well, too. I'll come back again someday James, when the time is right. I have no wish to confront my father."

Before we left James turned to me and said, "There are many changes coming. If you saw the lands to the east, you would know that soon there will be many people coming to the frontier—people like me."

"I know this. My Grandfather has said it, and many others have seen the lands covered with your people. But the land is so big. There is room for all of us, isn't there?"

He nodded. "There should be. I am glad to have met you, Little Chief. I will tell others what you have said about the Indian people. Take care of my brother."

"I will." And then I smiled. "Jonathan requires a great amount of care."

It took James a moment to realize I had made a joke. Mato Ska caught it and clipped my arm up near the shoulder.

James laughed and said, "Yes, I am just a little bit jealous, Jonathan. You have made a good life for yourself—with another brother. I will miss you." He hugged Jonathan and held him close for a moment. Both had tears in their eyes again, and I felt my own grow moist.

With a glance toward Emily, James said, "We better go back so Mother and Father don't come looking for us. They have planned a big celebration party for tomorrow night, an engagement party. Many relatives and friends are coming from about three hours south of here. If you plan to leave, you must be gone quickly. We will be married soon—very soon, I hope." And he gave Emily a quick kiss. She blushed and poked him in the chest.

Jonathan stepped up and took Emily in his arms and kissed her on the lips. She looked shocked, but he laughed and said, "I just wanted to kiss the bride—since I won't be at the wedding." He motioned to me and together we crossed the stream and, with a single wave goodbye, moved once again into the undergrowth to get our horses.

I heard James say to Emily, "They disappeared. My God, isn't that something?"

Except for one quick, crashing thunderstorm, the long ride back to the village was leisurely and peaceful. Mato Ska seemed much relieved to have finally talked to his brother, and to have made a firm decision to remain with the Lakota people. It was as if the storm inside of my brother had finally spent itself; the sun was now shining. We laughed and raced and talked, stopping often to hunt or fish and taking the time to build a proper fire and eat well.

Toward the end of the trip, we stopped at a place along a river where the banks widened and formed a pool. We caught so many fish we decided to bring them to Morning Dove to cook for Grandfather and Unci as well.

Grandfather was pleased to see us enter the village. I greeted Morning Dove first with a kiss and my bag full of fish, and then we went to Grandfather's tipi to tell him all we had seen and done. I was relieved to see Grandfather looking strong and alert again. He listened to our tale and asked many questions. Finally, he looked at Mato Ska and said, "So, you have made a decision?"

"Yes, I have decided to stay here. It is the right life for me. I need the sky above me, the earth below. I need the sound of frog and bird and cricket. It feeds me. I need to learn more from the grandmothers so I can be the best doctor I can be."

Grandfather eyed him carefully, smiled, and said, "Welcome home, Mato Ska." He looked at me. "Tonight—we celebrate."

25 I Have No Ears

Life in the village settled into a peaceful rhythm of sun rising and sun setting. I could never remember being this content. Mato Ska had decided to stay; my part of the white bear's story was finished and I was looking forward to being a father, a husband to Morning Dove. Her birthing time was near. I cornered Unci and forced her to tell me her suspicions—that we would soon have a daughter.

The feeling was one of completion. Yet a small part of me felt restless and unfinished, though I could not name the reason. I wandered the encampment, seeking that which was hidden. It made no sense—until the morning I awoke beside my wife and heard a commotion outside the tipi, the sound of a horse stamping and huffing. I had awakened early and lay there listening to the baby's heartbeat, speaking softly with Morning Dove.

"Sounds like somebody is preparing to leave," she whispered.

I rose and went out of the tipi. Outside, I saw Mato Ska talking to Grandfather. With a nod from Grandfather, Mato Ska hurried to his own tipi, gathered a bundle and a buffalo robe, tied them to his horse, and rode out of the village fast.

I hurried to cross the ground to Grandfather. "Where is Mato Ska going?"

Grandfather said, "He woke up early with a strong feeling about his brother, a feeling that he must go to him immediately. We prayed together and then I gave him permission to go."

"I have to catch up to him."

When I turned to leave Grandfather caught my arm and said, "Mato Ska wanted to go alone. He does not want you to come after him."

"But Grandfather, we have always done these things together, since the first." I was stunned, even hurt and confused. "I brought him here, Grandfather. I am the one who rescued him, who taught him to be strong."

"No, Little Chief. He wants to do this on his own." Grandfather said nothing more.

A spear of anger pierced me. I turned and hurried back to Morning Dove and explained what was happening. "I am going to ride and catch up with him."

"But Little Chief, Grandfather said no. He said Mato Ska is to make this journey alone."

"It is a foolish journey to make alone. It is safer for two. You know that. Pack me a bundle, Morning Dove, there is no time to waste."

I went to the edge of the village. The horses were some distance away and I signaled Wasaka to come. The horse cocked its ears, raised its head. I signaled again and he trotted across the grass to me. I returned to my tipi, rolled my robe and took the pack Morning Dove had prepared. Mato Ska was gaining distance from the village and I needed to hurry. When I bent to kiss Morning Dove, there were tears in her eyes.

"Why do you cry, Morning Dove?"

She smiled a thin smile. "I cry a lot these days, Little Chief. You know that. Go. Go to your brother. I will be fine."

"You understand why I must go after him?"

"No, but I accept."

I pulled her close and kissed her, and then bent and kissed the round of her belly. "Take care of my little one."

"I will."

I put the leather on Wasaka's mouth and led him to Grandfather's tipi. The old man was still standing where I'd left him, staring after Mato Ska. "I'm sorry, Grandfather. I have to go catch up with him. It is better with two of us. Safer."

Grandfather said, "I cannot stop you, Little Chief, but your brother wanted to go alone."

"I know, but I must go." I hesitated and said, "I had another dream about bears last night, Grandfather. I have had this dream before. It was much like the dream of the white bear, but in this dream there were black bears, many of them, and all had a band of *maza*, of metal around their bleeding necks. It disturbed me. It hurt my heart, just as the dream of the white bear hurt me."

Grandfather shook his head. "Enough, Little Chief. You went through enough with one white bear; you better leave these black bears for someone else to dream of rescuing. Concentrate on Mato Ska."

"Yes, Grandfather. But there is something I want to give you." I took the pouch from my hip, tipped it up, and rolled the small metal ball into my palm. I handed it to him. "This. I don't want to meet up with one of these. You can have this back."

Again, Grandfather said nothing. He took the round ball, cupped it in his hand, and stared at me as I mounted Wasaka and rode away. When I reached the edge of the village, I looked back. The tipis formed a large circle across the encampment, all the openings facing the council tipi, the smoke rising in thin trails above the crossed poles emerging from under the hides.

The urge to get off my horse and return to Morning Dove was powerful. Perhaps Grandfather was right; perhaps I was not supposed to accompany Mato Ska on this ride. The peaceful scene of the village, of my wife and baby, called out to me, but I ignored the pull, turned away, leaned over my horse's back and said, "Run, Wasaka. Run."

26 The Last Journey South

Mato Ska was far ahead now and it would take time to close the distance. I rode. Wasaka felt like flowing water beneath me, so smooth and easy was his gait. I fell into the rhythm of that ride, letting my mind recall each moment of the night I'd taken my feather; and then further back, to each event that had led me to the boy beside the creek, to the journeys we had taken, to this moment. I felt again that disembodied feeling, of cloud and smoke, of not occupying this body. If it had not been for the snort and huff of Wasaka, I would have felt invisible on the wide, open lands.

By midmorning I saw Mato Ska ahead. He'd stopped near a stream to water his horse and I rode up beside him.

Mato Ska's face was a mix of joy, anger and distress, a sky unsure of its own weather. "You followed me."

"I did."

"I told Grandfather I didn't want you to follow me."

"I disobeyed Grandfather." I grinned.

Mato Ska appeared to hold his stern anger for a moment, but could not. He smiled at me and said, "So you did. It is good to see you, Little Chief, but I didn't want to involve you further in this."

"Do you want me to leave?"

"Yes. No. I don't know." Mato Ska stroked his horse's back. "I may not be coming back, Little Chief."

"I know this, but it felt like my part in these doings was not over yet."

He studied me, saying nothing, clearly still warring with his own inner emotions. "Let's ride then."

We mounted our horses and rode toward the south. Mato Ska told me about the sudden feeling that something was wrong, that his brother was calling him back once again. "It is different this time, urgent. Something is wrong, Little Chief, I feel it."

Because of the urgency he sensed, we stopped to rest only in the darkest hours of night, not bothering to build a fire, and waking before the birds to ride again. So it was that we arrived once again at the steaming creek late in the morning, having made the journey in less than two days. We were tired. The horses were tired. I felt the grit of not enough sleep and too much trail dust on my face. I washed my face in the creek, amazed once more at the warmth of the water and the odd, mineral smell of it. I looked at Mato Ska. "What do you want to do?"

"I'll go ahead on foot. You stay with the horses. I will whistle if I need you."

He ran off into the underbrush. I stood and watched him go, clutching the leathers in my hand with a tight fist. It did not feel right. I had not come along to hold the horses but to help him in whatever he must face. I left our horses and followed. When I was close to him I tossed a small stone to let Mato Ska know I was there. He turned and signed for me to wait. He'd reached the bank along the creek where the tree was, where the path led to the cabin.

I came up silently behind him. We looked out and saw nothing. The homestead was oddly silent, although smoke rose from the chimney so we knew it was not abandoned. Mato Ska signed that he was unsure of what to do next.

Clearly there was no one about so I said aloud, "We wait. There will be some sign of what is happening. You are tired, Mato Ska. So I am. Why don't we take turns sleeping? I'll watch while you sleep first. Go ahead."

"Maybe I should go up there."

"Patience, Little Brother. Get some rest and I will watch."

Mato Ska stretched out on a grassy spot. The horses were downstream so we had no supplies with us. I positioned myself at the top of a small rise, still out of sight but with a clear view of the cabin. The sun baked the top of my head and the bees were buzzing in the wildflowers along the bank of the river. Within minutes, my head dropped and I dozed.

In the low hum of buzzing bees and wind blowing I suddenly heard another sound, a woman's voice. My head snapped up and I saw Emily racing down the path to the river. Mato Ska was already standing and looking in her direction. She was calling his name, both of his names.

"Jonathan? Where are you? Mato Ska? White Bear?"

Emily was upset, crying his name with a desperate note in her voice. Before I could caution him otherwise, he leapt out of the bushes and ran toward her. He reached the bank just as she came over the small rise. She saw him and ran immediately into his arms. She was sobbing. He stroked her back, called her name, and comforted her, and then he begged her to tell him what was wrong.

I saw no signs of the mother or father, or of James, so I too ran out of hiding, crossed the creek and came up to Mato Ska and Emily. I knew she would not be afraid of me. In fact, she looked at me, relief apparent in the glow of her eyes.

She calmed her sobs and took a deep breath and spoke finally, "I have been so afraid, Jonathan. Your parents . . . they are very sick. James rode away last night to get the medicine he needed in the city. He left me with them—but I don't know what to do. I'm afraid they will die."

Mato Ska shushed her. "Slow down, my dear. Tell us what happened, from the beginning."

Emily sniffed and wiped her eyes. "It was after the party, for our engagement. One of the guests must have brought a fever with them. Two days after the party, both your mother and father took sick; coughing, fever, chills. They are burning up, Jonathan. Your brother went to find medicine. Oh god, I didn't want to be alone with them. I'm a nurse, but I don't know enough to help them. James won't be back for two more days." Her hysteria was mounting again. "I was afraid he'd return and find them both dead."

Mato Ska straightened, looked at me, and said, "How did you know to call me?"

Emily looked confused, shook her head, and said, "I don't know, Jonathan. I don't know."

He nodded, "Come, we must go to them."

When we reached the cabin door, Emily stopped us. "What if both of you get sick too?"

Mato Ska said, "I can't help them if I don't go in, Emily. But we can lessen the risk. Go in and gather all the towels, sheets, their clothing; anything that may hide the sickness within it. Little Chief, you build a hot fire. Fill those cooking pots with water and we'll boil everything before using it again. I will go gather what I need. And Little Chief, when the fire is burning you go to the river and cut thin willow branches to build the frame for sweating. You need to . . ."

"I know what to do, Mato Ska. It is the same frame you and Unci put me under when I broke my arm. I know what to do."

He nodded and said, "Of course you do. So build the frame and choose the rocks to heat. I'll be back soon." He left without entering the cabin.

I hurried to build up the fire while Emily hauled all the clothing and bedding from the cabin. She dipped each piece into boiling water and hung it along a fence to dry. I felt shy with the young white girl, but she seemed so relieved to have help, to be given something constructive to do, that she was soon humming over her work. She looked up once and said in slow English, "How did you know to come?"

I said, "Mato Ska knew. He felt his brother calling his name."

Emily smiled and went back to her work. I carried wood from a stack near the corral, the same place I had watched Mato Ska's father pick up a stick and beat him so many years ago. The memory still hurt my heart, but now the angry man lay inside near the door of death. I determined to set aside such memories and do what was needed to help the white couple. There was nothing to fear from the man's thunder stick when he was laid so low with fever. I went down the stream and collected our horses and walked them up the slope. I left them eating grass beside the cabin.

When Mato Ska returned, I was finishing the fragile frame of willow branches. It was bent and tied with sinew. I tried to follow them into the cabin but Mato Ska put up a hand and stayed me. "I don't want you to get this sickness, Little Chief. Stay out here and tend the fire. You can watch from there."

I positioned myself near the open door where I could watch. Mato Ska directed Emily in helping him set the frame over his parents' bodies. He took the buffalo robes and carried them in. I prodded hot rocks into a kettle and set them on the stoop when Mato Ska was ready for them. Unsure of what else I could do to help, I took my flute and began playing, using the time to talk to *Wakan Tanka*, to ask the creator to come to their aid. I prayed, and played the music.

Mato Ska and Emily came and went, carrying buckets of water, entering the cabin again and again to tend the sick couple. I heard him describe to Emily each thing he was doing, instructing her on making the healing teas and broths, how to mash roots and leaves to make a poultice for their coughs, the need to bathe their fevered bodies with cold water after each round of sweating beneath the covered willow frame.

Emily's cheeks grew pink with exertion. Finally, when they had done all they could, they came and sat down, too tired to talk, and listened to me play my flute. Evening came and they took turns tending the sick couple, resting, sitting beside the fire and finally talking. Emily asked many questions. Mato Ska answered, telling her all about his life with the Lakota people. As much to distract her as to inform her, he told her of how I took him from where he was tied by the creek; of the gifts and learning he'd gained from the grandmothers; of my broken arm.

I caught enough of the English to feel ashamed again of how I'd tried to show off. Now it seemed like a long, long time ago and I realized I was finally more man than boy. I listened, feeling proud of the way Mato Ska described our village in such tender terms. He told her of happy children and gentle mothers, of great hunters, of how I got my feather—and of his hope that some day he would get his own feather.

We left the cabin door open all night, making rough beds beside the fire so we could doze when not tending to the sick couple. We kept this rhythm all that night, and all the next day, with Mato Ska and Emily going in and out of the cabin and me singing, praying, and playing my flute.

With not enough to do, I scouted around and found a discarded ring of metal that reminded me of the *maza*, the metal collars I'd seen the black bears wearing in my dream, only it was bigger than a neck. I took a piece of hide and strong, thick sinew and strung the hide across the metal frame. I took a thick cutting of willow and formed a stick, padding the end with bits of fabric from Emily's washing cloths. She sat beside me and watched, fascinated, as I created a small hand drum. Her eyes widened when I began to beat the drum with my stick and sing a healing song.

By the time I finished, tears were streaming from her eyes. "I have hurt you?" I asked in my rugged English.

"No, Little Chief. You have not hurt me. It is your music. It touched my heart."

I smiled. "Then it is a good thing, to touch a heart."

"Yes, it is a good thing."

I liked James's woman. I was happy I'd come to help Mato Ska and this girl fight against death. Although they tended the bodies, I felt I was tending the spirits of the parents and of Mato Ska and Emily. My flute, and the drumming and singing, provided a humming connection with *Wakan Tanka*. I felt it there, above the treetops, on the line between sky and earth, in the comings and goings in and out of the cabin.

By that evening, Mato Ska's parents were beginning to recover. The fevers were down and the shivering had lessened, although they still seemed to be walking in another world; unaware, unspeaking, as near to death as any human body could be. Mato Ska finally let me step through the door to see them.

"Their names are Heidi and Ryan Edwards."

I realized I'd never heard their names before. Mato Ska had never said them aloud. It was as if, in speaking their names aloud now, my friend and brother had re-entered the lives of his original family. It was an odd feeling, the parents suddenly more human than they had ever been in my mind. The dream of the white bear had so consumed me that I'd never even considered that I was removing a child from the home of his parents. It was right, I felt that, and yet it felt strange. Now it seemed I'd delivered their son back to them just in time to save their lives.

Life was strange. Maybe the realization that I would soon be a father was giving me a new view on things.

In the midst of these roaming thoughts, I saw Heidi open her eyes and look up at Emily. She glanced at Mato Ska, and then back to the girl. I saw that her mind was finally clearing of the fever. Heidi smiled a weak smile. Emily took her hand and asked, "How are you feeling, Mrs. Edwards?"

Heidi did not answer. She looked at Mato Ska. "Who is that?"

She could not see me from where she lay.

Emily paused, looked up at Mato Ska. I knew she was unsure of her place so she said, "You have been very ill. This man came to help."

Mato Ska stepped forward and touched Emily's shoulder. With a glance into his face, she stepped aside so he could approach his mother. He looked into Heidi's face and said softy, "It's Jonathan, Mother."

The fever-bright glaze in her eyes cleared and tears gathered there instead. "My son? Is it really you, Jonathan?"

"Yes, Mother. It's me."

"You're alive."

"I am. I've been living with the Lakota Indians these past years."

Perhaps out of long habit, or fear of her husband, I noticed her turning abruptly to see Ryan. He was still in the death-like state. "Your father?" she asked.

"I think he will be fine. He has not yet gained consciousness."

She sank back into the pillows again, a weary smile on her face. "Jonathan . . ." she said, then drifted back into sleep.

Emily stepped forward. "We should let her rest. She will probably think she dreamed you."

It was as much a suggestion as an observation. I knew she was saying Mato Ska could still go away, that his presence could yet go unnoticed if he chose to leave again. Mato Ska caught the inference. "I'm not leaving, Emily. I will wait for my brother to come, for my father to awaken."

We went back out into the cool evening air. I picked up my drum and thrummed it softly while Mato Ska and

Emily talked quietly together. The crisis had passed. Heidi and Ryan Edwards would survive this illness.

The next morning, it was as we had thought. Both were recovering. Emily expected James would return that day. She came out from the cabin and approached Mato Ska. "Your father is coming around. And your mother is awake again." Emily smiled. "She said she's hungry."

Mato Ska nodded. "A good sign. I'll go in." He glanced at me.

"I'll stay here. I can keep watch from the door."

"Thank you, Little Chief." He went into the cabin and approached their bed. I saw the slight hesitation, the holding back so that his father would not see him. And then he took a deep breath and stepped firmly to the bedside. The boy who had been tied to a tree, beaten with a stick, was still alive in Mato Ska. Out of long habit of watching out for Mato Ska, I stood near, out of Ryan's sight but able to watch—to know that my brother was all right.

Mato Ska approached his father's bed. The man, still weak, barely conscious, opened his eyes and looked up into the face of his son. "Who are you?"

"I am Jonathan, Father."

The man raised his hand and scrubbed it across his eyes and looked again. "Jonathan?"

"Yes, Father."

"You are dead."

Mato Ska laughed. "Not dead. Quite alive in fact."

"Where did you come from?"

"Initially, from you, I suppose. I've been living with the Lakota people, Father. I left."

"Savages?"

"No, Father. Not savages. A kind and gentle people." Before Mato Ska could say more, the man had fallen asleep again.

Heidi raised her hand and touched his arm. "He has been very sick, Jonathan. Give him some time."

Mato Ska nodded and came back out to where I waited.

"Your mother is right," I said. "He probably thinks he dreamed you."

"He has always wished I was only a dream." With those words, he turned and strode out across the yard toward the river.

I followed. When I caught up with Mato Ska at the bank of the river, the place where our story had first begun, my brother was picking up rocks and plunking them into the water. His body was tight, the anger and grief like a scent around him.

I said nothing, waiting for the storm of emotions to pass.

Finally Mato Ska turned and said, "I have always been a disappointment to him. That is why I left with you, Little Chief. I couldn't bear to see my own reflection in his eyes. I disliked what I was becoming around him. . . why won't he love me?"

Mato Ska's anger dissolved into anguish and I felt helpless to help my friend with this inner struggle. I had no answers for why a father would not love a son. I thought of the baby in Morning Dove's belly and knew already I loved that little one. There was no comfort I could offer, so I stood silent while Mato Ska curled onto the ground and wept and beat his fist against the earth.

When his anger and grief were spent, he raised his head again and rose. "No more, Little Chief. I will ask no more of him than the life he gave. It is enough." He turned and walked toward the cabin.

In the edge of my vision, I still saw the white bear of my dreams tied to that tree, his neck scabbed and bleeding—but his face peaceful. I remembered seeing the way Mato Ska had pushed his father to punish him. Later, I would remind Mato Ska that he, too, had made a choice. Later.

Emily met us as we neared the cabin again. "Your father is awake again, Jonathan. He wants to see you."

Mato Ska looked at me and said, "Come with me. It is time you met my father."

I expected to find an angry man lying in the bed, but the illness had softened his spirit. In fact, he was only an aging, unhappy man who had been very ill.

Mato Ska stood beside the bed. Ryan Edwards looked up at him. Heidi was sitting up, looking nearly recovered, and smiling. "Your father has something he wants to tell you."

With some struggle, Mato Ska's father pulled his weakened body upright and straightened his shoulders. He saw me for the first time and said, "Who is that?"

Mato Ska said, "My Lakota brother." His voice had an edge of defiance, as if he expected his father to use that word again. Savages.

Instead of responding in anger, however, the weary man said to me, "I fear you have been a better father to my son than I have."

I said nothing. I glanced at Mato Ska's shocked face.

Ryan put his hand on his son's arm. "There is nothing I can say to make up for how I treated you. I wanted you to be more like James. I thought punishing you would give you strength. I was wrong."

Mato Ska stared, saying nothing, waiting.

Ryan shook his head. "Look at you. You look like a dang injun."

I felt Mato Ska stiffen and stepped closer. But then Ryan said, "No . . . you look like a man." He looked at me and said, "You took a boy away and brought a man back with you."

The tension between mother and father, between father and son, dissolved with those words. Ryan again touched Mato Ska's arm. "I'm sorry, Son. Your mother tells me that I would not even be alive if not for your efforts. She says you have become a doctor after all. Bring a chair. Tell me about these Lakota people."

Heidi wept softly. I chose that moment to bow out of the room and let them attempt, once more, to become a family. Emily followed. Outside, I picked up the small drum and began singing a song of celebration. It seemed there was much to celebrate.

27 *Maza*—Spider Bite

The rest of the day was spent waiting for James to return. Heidi and Ryan tested their bed-weary legs with small walks in the sunshine. Ryan even made an effort to talk to me, to set aside his previous dark thoughts about Indians. Mato Ska spent long hours telling both his parents about the past five years and how the Lakota people lived. Heidi, in particular, wanted to know everything about the women, the grandmothers, how life was in a village such as ours. When she found out I was about to be a father, she congratulated me and went back inside to prepare a gift for me to take to my wife and child.

Toward evening, Ryan and Heidi had again taken to their bed to rest. Emily was making the evening meal and I sat on the stoop drumming and singing. Mato Ska added his voice to the song. The sun was fast dropping in the western sky when suddenly we heard riders coming in. There was a shout, a cry or call, and then the crack of the thunder stick, and then another and another.

The peace of the moment shattered with that terrible sound and the sight of the riders in blue coats coming fast. I was up and running for Wasaka. Too well I remembered that sound, that *maza*, that thunder, that metal ball. I reached Wasaka and mounted almost without thinking, heading east toward the low ridge of pine and thicket.

Emily screamed as the riders rode toward the cabin, rifles thundering. Mato Ska raced to his own horse and mounted, riding after me.

I raced forward, leaning into my horse's side to stay clear of flying metal. I glanced back, saw Mato Ska behind me, saw Emily rip her apron off and wave it, screaming at the soldiers to stop shooting. I saw Ryan and Heidi stumble out from the door of the cabin. Time seemed suddenly to be both slow as a sluggish river—and racing like thunderclouds. My only thought was to reach the protection of the forest ahead. The forest . . . the forest . . . reach the forest . . . drummed in my head in rhythm to Wasaka's galloping hooves. Behind me, Mato Ska screamed, "Ride, Little Chief, ride!"

The horses of the strangers thundered nearer. Suddenly, I felt a sharp sting in my back, just below the shoulder blade and my chest flamed into pain. My ears pounded with the beating of my own heart, with Wasaka's heart and then, as if time were slowing . . . slowing . . . slowing . . . I heard Wasaka's heart beating, but the sound seemed to withdraw from me. Dazed and weak, my hearing dimmed, my view of the tree line ahead grew hazy and blurred. I heard Mato Ska scream "No! No!" behind me but it sounded far away, so distant and faint. I tried to look behind me, but the motion increased my dizziness. I lost my hold on Wasaka and slid off, hitting the ground and rolling onto my back.

I knew then that I'd ridden Wasaka for the last time; that I would not return alive to my village; that the *maza*, the spider, had bitten me. My chest burned and it was hard to breathe but my senses felt keen, alert. I heard the soldiers thunder up and stop. I heard Mato Ska slide from his horse and come to my side. I smelled earth, and dust, and sage and pine. I smelled evening sun. I smelled blood.

Mato Ska screamed at the soldiers. "You shot him. Why did you shoot him? He is my friend, my brother. You shot my brother." James got off his horse and tried to explain, that the soldiers thought the homestead under attack, that he had had no time to explain.

Mato Ska did not hear his brother. He was crying my name when he fell to the ground beside me. "Little Chief, don't die. Hang on. We will carry you to the house. I can make you well."

My tongue felt thick in my mouth and I was suddenly thirsty. I didn't want to die, didn't want to miss the birth of my child, or the sight of my wife with our babe at her breast. I closed my eyes, squeezed them tight against the pain in my body. When I opened them again, I saw the brilliant setting sun like flames behind the soldiers—behind Mato Ska. Emily, James, and his parents were all standing there, too. "Mato Ska, hear me," I whispered.

He kneeled and leaned close. "What, Little Chief?" he said. "Don't die, my brother. You will not die. I will not let you die."

"Shut up, Mato Ska, and listen. I will not be going home alive. I feel this. Tell Morning Dove and my daughter, tell Grandfather and my parents, of my great love for them."

Mato Ska cried, the tears streaking the dust of his face. His yellow hair looked like flame against the orange of the sun's rays. He tried to smile.

"Don't cry, Mato Ska. I can be killed, but I will return one day." My voice was growing weaker. There was not much time. "Do you remember when Grandfather took us to the butte shaped like a bear, or a pregnant woman, the place twins come from?"

"Yes, I remember."

"Tell Grandfather I want my scaffold placed there, where we prayed, where the wind can carry my ashes to the east. Tell them I want my body burned, to be sure I do not carry the illness to my people. Tell him, Mato Ska."

"I will tell him."

"And put my feather in Wasaka's mane, tie it there, and let him go free again."

"I understand, Little Chief. Oh god, please don't go. What will I do without you?"

I looked once more into Mato Ska's face. "You will do what you have to do, *Kola*. You will do what *Wakan Tanka* wants you to do. But I fear my end is only the beginning of more death, my brother. Grandfather spoke it and now it has arrived."

"No. I will tell them, Little Chief. I will tell them the Lakota people are not warriors—they are hunters. I will make them listen, Little Chief."

"They have no ears to hear you, Mato Ska."

28 The Final Journey Home

The dying was a peaceful thing after all. The beating of my heart grew dim, as if the earth were taking it into her self, absorbing my life into her gentle body. I felt my breathing slow, the air filling my lungs once, again more slowly, and then, a final exhale.

The rising above was the most beautiful moment I'd ever experienced; the merging with sun and pine, the lifting to the realm of eagles and spirit, the waft and lift of wind, the loss of the constraint of skin and bone and flesh, and the widening out, the embrace of something much, much larger. I no longer needed air—I was air.

I hadn't expected to still have use of ears and memory when my body was shed—left to return again to the earth— but I heard Emily crying, heard Mato Ska exhale even as I breathed my last. Heidi wept too, telling the soldiers how Mato Ska and I had saved their lives.

They carried my body to the front of the cabin where I had spent so many long hours singing and praying—as if I'd known and wanted to make sure *Wakan Tanka* knew where I was and could claim me the moment my spirit left this body. Yes, I saw . . . I heard . . .but I could do nothing to comfort those left behind. Emily and Heidi washed my bleeding body with cold cloths, and their own tears. They laid me out before the fire I'd tended and placed my flute on my chest, my bow and arrow beside me. Wasaka was already stamping and huffing, already returning to his own freedom. I made the familiar noise to signal him and Wasaka raised his ears to look. My horse, at least, could still hear me.

When my body had been cleansed and prepared, Mato Ska picked up the small, metal-rimmed drum that looked so like the collars I'd seen in my dream. He picked up the drum and began to sing in Lakota, a song of mourning and honor, a song of bravery and love. I thought Mato Ska had never sung so well. His song reached all the four corners of the world. I was sure my Grandfather heard that song, and Morning Dove, and my parents. I was sure that song would echo on for a hundred years, maybe more, until others heard it, too. Wasaka had heard my call. Perhaps Mato Ska could feel me as well. There was no hand within my control, no body, but I imagined placing a hand over Mato Ska's heart and holding it there, the way I sometimes felt *Wakan Tanka* touch my heart. It pleased me when my brother paused, as if listening, his face softening, the grief lessening. I realized *Wakan Tanka* can touch a heart—and I was now being breathed in by *Wakan Tanka*.

When Mato Ska finished the song, he looked up to find the soldiers had removed their hats. The women still wept; his father stood beside him holding his elbow. Mato Ska said, "I have to take Little Chief back to his people now. I don't know what will happen. I will take him alone." He looked at the soldiers. "Do not follow."

Mato Ska didn't wait for morning. He didn't wait for permission. He didn't even wait while the soldiers conferred with the commander, agreeing not to follow. Instead, he asked James to help him roll my body into my buffalo robe and secure it to Wasaka's back. He hugged his mother, kissed Emily, looked long at his father through his tears, and then asked James to ride with him part of the way. Heidi tried to stop him, insisting she must pack him some food, but he declined her offer. He told her that he knew the land well and could feed himself.

216

Before the sun disappeared behind the horizon, Mato Ska left the homestead with my lifeless body on Wasaka, James silent beside him. His brother rode along for an hour until Mato Ska said, "This is far enough. Go back to Emily, James. I will continue on to the village alone."

"I hate to leave you. What will happen, Jonathan?"

"Things will change. The people will not take this action lightly. Grandfather has seen the way the world is changing. He has been preparing the people for this time."

"Will you stay with them?" James asked.

"I don't know. I might stay; I might return. Or perhaps I'll find a place of my own to be."

My spirit lingered with my body, listening, taking in the conversation of the twin brothers. I felt no connection to the dead body slung across Wasaka. That part of my time on earth was gone and yet I could not leave. Grandfather had not told me what to do once my spirit had separated from my body, so I made the journey with Mato Ska.

James turned back toward the homestead and Mato Ska watched him go. There were tears in his eyes and I knew my friend was mourning this day, wishing he'd insisted I not follow him. His heart had spoken, had foreseen the terrible day, but he had not listened. Grandfather had warned me not to go. I had not listened.

Mato Ska rode with deadly determination, not racing, but barely stopping either. All day and late into the night he traveled, pausing only for short periods. Even then, he did not rest but busied himself shooing the flies from the body draped across Wasaka. By evening the next day, he was nearing the village.

I felt Mato Ska's reluctance to enter the village. A scout in the distance disappeared to report the arrival of riders. Then he returned to watch two horses—one rider—approach. Although I felt my spirit tethered to Mato Ska and the body on Wasaka, I could also see into the village. I saw expectant faces, heard the sudden silence as the children halted their games, felt the women pause in their evening chores.

And I felt Morning Dove. She knew. I saw her slip into the tipi and return with a bundle. She'd had our baby—and already she knew that the child in her arms had lost her father. I felt her heart thud with pain, the tears filling her eyes, the cry gathering in her throat.

When Mato Ska rode into the village, all of the people had gathered near the river. Grandfather Whirling Hand stepped forward. Mato Ska said nothing. He slid off his horse, walked both horses to Grandfather and handed him Wasaka's rein. At last he spoke, "I have brought your grandson home."

"What has happened, Mato Ska?" Grandfather asked.

"When we got to my father's house, we found both my mother and father near death from a fever. My twin brother had gone for medicine. Little Chief and I tended them. They had nearly recovered when the soldiers came. The soldiers didn't stop to ask questions . . . they shot him."

The people gasped, almost a single sound emanating from a single throat. Morning Dove held the baby tighter, but refused to cry. She wanted to hear every word Mato Ska said. When Rabbit stepped forward, his eyes on the body laid over Wasaka, Mato Ska couldn't look. He hung his head, and said, "The soldiers came with my brother, James."

I had not realized my friend and brother felt responsible until he spoke those words. Mato Ska blamed himself for that lifeless body on Wasaka. Rabbit stepped next to Mato Ska and touched his shoulder—I loved my childhood friend even more in that moment.

Grandfather shook his head. "He chose to go with you, my grandson. The decision was his. You, and I too, felt you should go alone."

Mato Ska choked back tears but regained his poise. "Little Chief wants his body taken to Bear Mountain, to the place we prayed. He wants it placed on a scaffold and burned where the wind will take his ashes and carry them east. He told me this before he died. He also said he wants no other hunter to ride Wasaka. We are to tie his feather in Wasaka's mane and free him." Mato Ska spoke without expression, saying the words that needed to be said. He turned to Morning Dove, "Little Chief said to tell his parents, and you Grandfather, and Morning Dove, that he loved you all very much and carries that love with him to the next realm."

With those words, Morning Dove's rigid body crumpled to the ground. Unci and my mother flew to her side, taking the baby, taking her in their arms, absorbing her grief into their own bodies.

Grandfather touched Mato Ska's arm. "Thank you for bringing Little Chief home."

Mato Ska said, his throat thick with grief, "I am sorry to bring him home this way."

I watched the village mourn my death. With my spirit no longer in my body, I felt no connection to the sadness, only to the love. I was proud of Mato Ska, proud of Morning Dove, proud of the way the women sheltered and comforted her and my infant daughter. It was this love that would sustain them, which would carry them through the coming changes, which would buffer every blow. It seemed odd how I had never fully realized this, the sustaining power of love, in life—only in death.

Grandfather sent the people back to their tipis and put my body in the care of Unci and the other grandmothers. They prepared my body for its final journey. Morning Dove insisted on helping. When my body was cleansed and prepared, she took our daughter and sat down on the earth to nurse her. Grandfather crossed the open area and sat down beside her.

He asked, "Your daughter, does she have a name yet?"

Morning Dove smiled through her tears. "Yes. Little Chief named her. He knew the baby was a girl. He said he coerced Unci into telling him. Unci told him that when the baby rides low, it is a girl; when it rides high, it is a boy. This one rode very low."

"What is her name, Granddaughter?"

"Little Chief said her name was to be 'Shining In The Water.'"

"And does this name have a meaning for you and Little Chief?"

"It does, Grandfather. One night when the moon was full and bright, Little Chief went to water his horse and he saw, below the surface of the river, something shining in the moonlight. He said he wanted to pluck the shining thing out of the water but something stopped him." Morning Dove's cheeks were wet with tears, but she went on. "He came and got me and made me stand a certain way to catch the glint; it was like a small fire on the river bottom. When I leaned forward to reach for it, he stopped me and told me no, this shining thing belongs to the water, to the earth, and should not be plucked out."

Grandfather sighed. "Ah. It is the *maza*, the metal that brings the Others. They seek it." He seemed to consider the baby's name for a while and then said, "Your husband, Morning Dove, had strong vision. Even as a young boy, he was guided by *Wakan Tanka*, by his dreams. It was his vision of the white bear that led him to Mato Ska, and it was his vision that led him to his death. We can't understand these things, Granddaughter. We can only accept that *Wakan Tanka* understands and acts in our behalf."

"Yes, Grandfather. I know this. But in this moment, I'm not sure I accept it."

Grandfather kissed her brow and said, "Tomorrow we take Little Chief to Bear Mountain."

Late that night, as the moon rose and the sky turned into a muddy dark blanket above the camp, I took my spirit to my favorite place on the upper hillside to pray and watch. What I saw down there disturbed me.

Already the young hunters spoke in anger, spoke of revenge. The women, normally peaceful and contented, were agitated, afraid, whispering together of Grandfather's announcement—that tomorrow they would go to Bear Mountain—and then the village must divide into smaller bands and travel separately.

Grandfather moved from group to group consoling, offering wisdom, reminding the angry men. He reminded them that their first priority was to protect the elderly and the women and children—and not to ride off and make war.

I saw that my death was like lightning striking the crisp, dry grasses of autumn. It had ignited them, set them on fire, sent the first flames dancing across the prairies. I raised my eyes and looked above the village to the expanding lands beyond and was shocked to realize I could see time passing, people moving, wagons coming, soldiers coming. I saw my people scattered and moving across the land, propelled by fear and anger.

My vision—no longer constrained by physical eyes— saw far, far beyond, into the future and back to the past, saw above it all. What I saw nearly crushed my spirit. It was then I heard the voices singing, many voices; the voices of my ancestors, of *Wakan Tanka*, of my daughter now grown into a woman. It seemed as if time itself collapsed and I heard and saw all things at once.

I added my own spirit voice to the singing and it soothed, reminding me that I am Lakota still, even in death, and reminding me that as long as the singing continues, the Lakota people will go on.

"I'll be back," I added to the song. "I will return."

Ash

For the next many days, the singing continued, carried by wind and wing and spore to all the corners of the earth. The people traveled and carried my body to Bear Butte and laid me high up on the scaffold. They prayed, and wept, and sang. When the fire touched the wood stacked beneath the scaffold and crawled up to consume my remains, I felt an explosion as my body blackened, and crumbled and became ash. The ash was carried into song and wind, an eastern wind.

I am ash now.

My feather was tied in Wasaka's mane and the horse, his heart beating fast, raced off following ash and wind, moving east. I felt myself on Wasaka's back once again, the horse's heartbeat merging with mine for just a moment . . . and then gone. Gone to the winds. Gone to the east. Gone to the other realms.

Wasaka was free.

I was free.

About Jamie Lee

Jamie Lee has been writing and teaching for the past twenty years. Her love of the land—and of people—shows in both her fiction and nonfiction. Jamie currently teaches at Oglala Lakota College located on the Pine Ridge Reservation.. She has presented workshops in creative writing, communications, and Family Constellation Work for many years.

Jamie and her husband, Milt Lee have produced over 70 documentary programs for public radio including a landmark public radio series called *Oyate Ta Olowan—The Songs of the People* which features more than fifty Native American tribes. She grew up in Northern Minnesota and currently lives in Rapid City, SD.

About Leon Hale

Leon Hale was born in Thunder Butte, SD on July 20, 1954. He and his wife Priscilla have two children and seven grandchildren. They currently live in Rapid City on the edge of the Black Hills. Leon has worked as a carpenter most of his life and now volunteers his skill to Head Start and other worthy projects.

A Note From Leon Hale

I had a dream and I would like to share it in this story so everybody can read it to the Elderly and the young ones. It is mostly about my Lakota people and how we used to help each other and live when we were living in tipis. Back then the Grandmothers and Grandfathers were our teachers and they taught us our cultural ways, about living, sharing, and respecting Mother Nature and giving thanks to Wakan Tanka (God) who created this land we live on.

Our busy fathers and uncles hunted for food and our mothers and aunts cooked and made clothes for us to keep warm. They also taught what they knew to the younger ones.

We were strong, powerful Lakota people with many great chiefs and warriors. Our Grandfathers Crazy Horse and Sitting Bull were strong leaders. This is why I wanted to title this book *Washaka*. It means "strong," which we will be again if we listen to and respect our Elders, and work together in a good way.

Leon Hale and Jamie Lee welcome your letters and thoughts on *Washaka—The Bear Dreamer.*
Send comments to jamie@manykites.com

Many Kites Press

Other Books by Jamie Lee

*Re-Visioning Adolescence
and the Rite of Passage*, nonfiction, $12.95

Feeling Good About Feeling Bad,
Nonfiction $11.95

Other titles from Many Kites Press

Systemic Constellation Work is an Art—A collection of Essays
by Heinz Stark, $12.95

Cinder and Mr. B, a children's book
by Mary Hadley, $12.95

Wicoicage—The Future, collected student writings from
Oglala Lakota College. $10.99

*On Love and Other Things, A Conversation
With Bert Hellinger*—a double CD audio set. $24.95

Many Kites Press is associated with Oyate.com which
features over 60 audio and film products on Native
American music and topics. See www.oyate.com

To order any of these titles using a credit card,
or to ask about wholesale rates
Call 1 (800) 486-8940
www.manykites.com

Order Form

To order, copy the form below and mail to:
Many Kites Press, 3907 Minnekahta Dr., Rapid City, SD 57702
or call 1 (800) 486-8940

Title	Price	S & H	Total
Washaka—The Bear Dreamer, by Jamie Lee	$12.95	$3.00	
Re-Visioning Adolescence and the Rite of Passage, by Jamie Lee	$14.95	$3.00	
Systemic Constellation Work is an Art, by Heinz Stark	$12.95	$3.00	
Cinder and Mr. B, by Mary Hadley	$12.95	$3.00	
On Love and Other Things: A Conversation with Bert Hellinger (double CD audio book)	$24.95	$3.00	
Wicoicage: The Future, Collected student writings From Oglala Lakota College	$10.99	$3.00	
Total due			

Ship To:

Name	
Address 1	
Address 2	
City	
State	Zip
Email address	
Visa MC Discover AMEX (circle one)	
Card #	
Exp. Date	
Last three #s near signature	
Signature:	